IN
OTHER
HANDS

Revised Edition

George Thomas Clark

Published by GeorgeThomasClark.com

ISBN: 978-0-9910623-4-8 – Trade Paperback

GeorgeThomasClark.com
Bakersfield, California
webmaster@GeorgeThomasClark.com

Books by George Thomas Clark

They Make Movies
Paint it Blue
Hitler Here
The Bold Investor
Basketball and Football
Down Goes Trump
King Donald
Death in the Ring
Echoes from Saddam Hussein
Obama on Edge
Tales of Romance
In Other Hands: Revised Edition

Introduction

In search of stimulating stories, I interviewed prostitutes in Madrid, Mexico City, Havana, and Managua and on many boulevards in the United States, and talked to detectives and rode the rough roads of social workers who deal with human trafficking, which is contemporary slavery, and sometimes used several lives to create stories, and everywhere I ventured I witnessed struggles of those whose lives are bound *In Other Hands*.

This revised edition includes *Where Will We Sleep*, which is also available in a separate edition, including an audio format.

Contents

IN OTHER HANDS

HUMAN TRAFFICKING

In the USA

In Foreign Lands

PROSTITUTION

Latin Flavor

Illegal

Legal

WHERE WILL WE SLEEP?

POVERTY

Homeless

Restless

On the Move

Contrasts

HUMAN TRAFFICKING

IN THE USA

Escape from Bondage

I was born in Ridgecrest, out in the desert two hours from Bakersfield. There's a lot of meth there and not much to do. My mom smoked and snorted it and was using all the time when I was a child but careful not to let me see her. I loved her but was hungry for attention. She and her live-in boyfriend were always in their bedroom. Neither one of them was working. They were typical tweakers, dealing meth, and would steal from anyone, even a child. Her boyfriend used to beat me with his belt, burn me with cigarettes, and call me fat. We didn't have the best diet. I remember eating noodles and garlic almost every day.

When I was seven-years old my mom got pregnant. My sister was born early and had to stay in the hospital five weeks. Child Protective Services showed up at my mom's and told me we were going to lunch, but they took me into custody and soon my little sister, too. Then we lived with a nice Baptist family but they wouldn't let me see my mom if I cried. My mom got clean and got us back a few months later, but she stayed with her boyfriend, my sister's dad, until I was ten. He was horrible, throwing glasses and cups all the time. And he started licking my face and forehead and made me sick with his nasty speed breath.

When my mom kicked her boyfriend out, her sister's husband, my uncle, started spending more time with us. He was a meth addict. He shot it, and he'd slap my butt and touch me in private areas and make nasty comments. I was scared. He beat my aunt so bad she's legally blind and deaf. Finally, when I was twelve, I got the courage to speak out and say, "Hey, Uncle Mike's been touching me." My mom called the police. They asked me to tell my story many times. I was always consistent, and my uncle went to prison for three years.

I started using meth when I was eleven. I was in a drug house and it was natural to just start snorting, three or four days a week. I'd go to school loaded. I didn't care. I had a lot of anger. I'd punch myself. I couldn't study. I'd ditch school and go smoke cigarettes and weed and drink alcohol and take more meth. Sometimes I could go a month or two without using but I always started again. In sixth grade I stopped going to school. By the time I was fifteen, I was a full-blown meth addict, shooting it as well as snorting and smoking. I liked it. My whole body felt high like my sternum was being pulled up and I was floating, super high. I felt invincible. The crashes were really bad. My whole body hurt when I wasn't high. I got so I picked at myself, my face, everywhere. I had a lot of cuts and scabs. It was a crazy life. I was hanging out with addicts in their thirties and forties. We sold drugs to make money.

Around this time I met a guy who became my boyfriend. We married when I was nineteen. We were both shooting meth and beating hell out of each other. The cops came so many times they stopped coming. My husband and I still loved each other. He came from a bad family and had been in and out of prison a lot for drug-related crimes. I found out I was pregnant ten weeks in and stopped using drugs. We had our daughter, Autumn, when I was twenty. After that I started sleeping with guys for drugs and money. Everything was crazy at home. The last time my husband beat me he almost ripped my ear off, and I had him jailed.

I was twenty-three and felt dead, with a puny little soul. I asked my mom to keep Autumn so I could leave town with a guy. He was twenty-one years older and sold meth but I didn't think about that. He painted a façade. I thought, "I won't have to fight this one." We got a ride from Ridgecrest to Bakersfield and took a bus to Reno. In Sacramento, he left my suitcase on the bus. Two hours after we got to Reno, he said, "If you want to eat, and sleep inside, you've got to earn some money."

It was winter and really cold in the mountains. The first two nights we slept outside. He told me, "Why give it away when you can get paid for it?" I felt it was okay, even when he said, "You've got to take care of us."

We fought all the time. Sometimes I'd hit him – I'm pretty big and can take quite a few guys – but he was very big and I did what he said. I'd go to truck stops and say to the drivers, "Hi, you want to buy some condoms? You want to party?" I'd get forty to sixty dollars for a quickie in their trucks. I was pretty friendly in casinos and met a man with rich friends. They'd take me to motels and I'd get a hundred fifty for fifteen minutes. My boyfriend was always watching and using his size to make sure he got paid. After four months of this, spinning out on alcohol and meth, I met a man who drove me to Portola, where I rested a few days, and then he took me to San Jose. He was a chemist and made meth at work and also bought it on the street.

I then met a guy who was a real gangster. He'd done fifteen years in prison for murder. He sold crack and meth as well as girls. He had about twenty-five girls all over, San Jose, Vegas, Chicago, Texas. He never slept with his girls or used drugs. It was all business. We lived on the second floor of a fairly nice apartment in the hood in San Jose. My name became Cash. No one called me Janet. I was one of his bottom girls. I worked for him a long time. We were friends. He told me, "I'm not going to beat your ass because if you're bruised I can't sell you." Sometimes he'd point his gun at my head and laugh. He also had hit men working for him.

A lot of the johns were really weird. Some dressed as women and did a lot of other things I wouldn't want to go into detail about. I wasn't scared of nothing. My husband had beaten me up for years. I felt I had incredible strength. But my pimp never gave me any money. He got everything. He just gave me drugs and clothes and drove me everywhere. If he had business somewhere else, he'd drop me off at places where people watched me until he got back.

One night in the apartment I felt like I was going to die. I didn't have any ID. He'd taken that and everything else. He told me to clean my room. I knew he'd kill me if I tried to leave. He gave drugs to people in the apartments around us so they'd watch me and the other girls. That night – it was March tenth last year – something kicked in. I'd just taken a shower and put on a dress. My hair was still wet – it was bright pink – and I wasn't wearing shoes. I opened the window and jumped from the second story. I was horrified and ran as fast as I could. In front of a church I saw a guy and started talking to him. My pimp kept calling over and over and over until my phone burned out. I had about thirty dollars from hiding five dollars here and there.

I walked around with the guy I'd just met, and we got a sack of meth and shot it up. It's twenty dollars a quarter gram if you don't know the dealers, and twenty for two grams if you know them. I needed money and had a date scheduled with a man but couldn't go there or my pimp would get me. I was tripping out on the guy I was with, and thinking about my pimp. I met another guy and stayed with him two days. He gave me a bicycle. I rode to downtown San Jose and went in a bathroom. When I came out, there's my pimp. He'd been texting my photo all over town and someone had called him. He said, "Where's my stuff, bitch?"

I jumped on my bike. He chased me but I rode over some light rail tracks and got away, but I kept seeing my photo on phones everywhere. I stole food from a market because I hadn't eaten in so long. A couple of days later I saw another hooker and she must've called my pimp. I was in front of a fast food restaurant when he saw me and said, "What the hell? You gotta make me some money."

I knew I was going to die. Guys like him will break all your bones and throw you where no one will ever find you. I couldn't talk to my family and couldn't see my kid. I was broken. Someone called him and he drove away. I cried out to God. I knew I'd had enough. I was in front of the Free Bird Café when an old man stopped and asked what was wrong. He must've been about eighty. He said, "Put your bike in my car." He took me to his house, a very nice place, and paid me three hundred dollars for a date.

I called the chemist in San Jose and took a bus to his house. I slept there a couple days straight, and he finally said, "I'm going to take you to Ridgecrest."

My mom's got eighteen years clean. When she saw me she wouldn't let me see my kid. I ran amok for about three days, using meth, alcohol, and weed. The police detained me for public intoxication. I think they didn't arrest me because I admitted I was high. That was March seventeenth last year and the last time I've used. I'm proud to have one year clean. But for a few days I had to stay at a place near my mom's house, and I could hear my daughter playing in the yard but couldn't visit her. When I gave my mom a clean drug test, she let me see Autumn.

On March twenty-eighth, when I'd been clean eleven days, we went to see the movie *The Trafficked Life*. My mom had heard of about it and a ministry run by Pastor Doug. He was there and so was the film's director and some girls who'd worked on the streets. There was a panel discussion afterward, and my mom stood in the crowd and said, "My daughter's being trafficked."

The pastor asked, "Are you ready to commit? Are you ready to change your life?"

I had to stay eighteen days in a secure domestic violence facility in Ridgecrest before I qualified to go to the restoration ranch run by the ministry. I started there April eighteenth. It's harder to change my life than stay in it but I've given myself to Christ. We have bible studies, AA meetings, and I've been taking college courses online. In June I'll have my associate's degree in Christian counseling. My grade point average is almost four-point-oh. Next, I plan to study the culinary arts. I love to cook. That's my passion.

Pink Van on Union Avenue

Sixty years ago Union Avenue was a small-town stretch of Highway 99 crowned by the yellow and blue Bakersfield sign and attracted vacationing stars such as Clark Gable, who stayed at the Bakersfield Inn, and working comedians like Johnny Carson, who reputedly bombed one night before rich cowboys and their brides in the club at Maison Jaussaud's restaurant. The Bakersfield Inn is currently a mundane motel located elsewhere and the original site a partially-boarded place you'd better approach carefully. The restaurant where Carson and other notables performed is now called the Golden West Casino and no longer attracts celebrities. Those who live on the arid plain of Bakersfield, breathing the nation's dirtiest air, either avoid Union Avenue or drive by ragged motels, darkened saloons, fast food joints, a cut-rate Food Maxx, used car lots, a dusty flea market, and businesses most don't notice. From the north, near 19th Street and Aldo's nightclub and a McDonald's, to Ming Avenue in the south there runs a strip walked by desperate women, most of whom are being watched by the snake eyes of their owners, euphemistically called pimps.

Tonight, I'm going to cruise Union with members of a ministry dedicated to helping women extricate themselves from the sex trade, which includes pornography and stripping as well as prostitution and sex trafficking. Before the journey, about forty people gather in the spacious northeast Bakersfield home of Pastor Doug. While this stocky and tattooed man stands on the patio next to the swimming pool, grilling hot dogs wrapped in bacon, I talk to a retired nurse who does volunteer work.

"We have a women's safe shelter in the mountains far from here," she says. "Their pimps can't find them there and they have a chance to recover. I often go up there to relieve the regular worker."

"Do you have a lot of activities for the women?"

"Yes, they do chores, and we have bible studies, and they can take college courses either online or in class. Sometimes I take them out for girlie things, manicures, hairstyling, movies."

"I heard you say you're sixty-eight. You look pretty good."

"That's right," she says. "Black don't crack."

As I mingle I meet a retired teacher, a social worker, a sports columnist, an electrician, and others, and listen to several young women discussing their jobs and college studies. People serve themselves informally, and I regret I've just eaten and forgo the wiener but can't resist a piece of chocolate cake for someone's birthday. After dining, everyone receives three sheets of lyrics to religious songs led by the adept vocals and guitar playing of a young blond lady. A female reporter and her cameraman arrive from a local television station to add to footage they've been filming for weeks. It's eighty-thirty now, two and a half hours after the party started, and Doug says, "Okay, let's load up the sacks for the women."

"What's in them?" I ask.

Two ladies combine to answer: "Tampons, toothbrushes, toothpaste, noodles, shampoo, conditioner, Valentine's candy, and other helpful items."

There are forty bags, twenty for each of the two vehicles slated to cruise tonight. I help load the ministry's long pink van decorated on the side by an image of a scantily clad young woman.

"Am I going in the van?" I ask Doug.

"Yes. Those in the SUV will be going to motels to talk to the women there. If the doors are open, that means they're open for business. We don't knock on closed doors. Our most experienced people go to the motels. In the van we'll talk to the women on the street."

Ten people climb into the pink van and disperse into four rows. On the way to Union Avenue, a few miles to the south, each person is called on to say a prayer. Perhaps sensing I'm not a religious scholar, Doug doesn't ask me to speak. The prayers stop when we reach Union. A little south of 19th Street, Doug pulls over next to a woman walking north on the sidewalk.

Patti, a young lady with long, curly red hair, from her front seat powers down the window and says, "Hi, can I offer you a gift?"

"Yeah."

She hands the woman a sack and asks, "Can I offer you a prayer?"

"Okay."

"What's your name?"

"Linda."

Patti holds the lady's hand and says, "What would you like to pray about?"

"I'm confused right now." They pray and say goodbye.

A young lady assigned to be the "scribe" types information into a small electronic tablet, and Doug, Patti, and others discuss whether this lady is being trafficked. They decide she is. Doug guides the van south and within two minutes turns right off Union and stops in the middle of the side street.

"Hi, can I offer you a free gift?" Patti asks.

The lady accepts the gift and the offer of prayer, and says, "My fiancé's in jail. I pray for protection and the wisdom to not end up in jail."

"There's her pimp," Doug says, pointing to a man lurking in a dark spot twenty feet away.

"That's the only lady in the street I've ever seen with a boob job," sounds a female voice. "She's huge. I think she's had a butt job as well."

Several passengers concur with these points of praise.

The next lady we approach prays for a job to get her off the streets. Afterward, the verdict is she's also being trafficked.

"I've seen that guy around here a few times," Doug says of a young motorist. "He just did a three-sixty (turn) in the parking lot of that motel. I'm going to follow him."

The car heads south on Union about a half mile before getting in the turn lane and making a U-turn, which Doug replicates, and heads north before turning right and moving into another motel. Passengers debate whether he's renting two motels for his prostitutes or doing something else. The pink van next moves to a lady who accepts the package but declines the prayer.

"I'm not a hooker," she says.

Nearby slithers a pimp.

Shortly, Patti talks to another lady who walks away, saying, "No thanks. I'm not a whore."

Driving again, Doug says, "It's Friday night on Union Avenue. They're all working. Jesus."

"I hold their hand the whole time we're talking and praying," says Patti, who references some of her experiences on the street. I haven't known about her history, and begin wondering about the five other young ladies in the van. "Did you also work like this?" I almost ask.

Two of the ladies, perhaps sensing uncertainty, inquire, "How are you doing, Tom? You okay?"

"I'm fine except I ate too much cake and cookies."

In a few minutes Doug guides the van beside a middle-aged lady in distress. She rambles about rushing to Idaho and then having to come back. I'm in the third row back and can't hear everything. As we leave, one of the ladies says, "She's broken."

Next we ease over and talk to a woman carrying something alternately flashing red, blue, and green. "What's that?"

"A speaker," she says, caressing her advertising aid.

Doug spots a lady he knows and pulls up to the locked wrought-iron gates of a fleabag motel.

"You can't park here," she says.

He drives around the corner and parks. Patti, a former police officer, and Doug take several bags, exit the vehicle, and walk toward the motel. I want to come but decide not to be a difficult guest. Several minutes later Doug excitedly returns and says, "Sheila lives in the same room where a prostitute shot me with heroin when I was twenty. We had a great reunion with several ladies in the parking lot, holding hands and praying. One was seventy years old. I've known her quite a while."

"What can a woman her age do out here?" I ask.

"Some men like them old, others like pregnant women, fat women, cross-dressers, everything."

Shortly, Patti passes out the final bag to a lady who declines prayer. She doesn't have time. Her pimp has appeared, growling and speaking unintelligibly.

It's about ten p.m., unofficial deadline for the pink van on Union Avenue, and we cruise up the hill to the northeast and disembark at Doug's house for debriefing.

I approach a man and softly ask, "Were all those girls in the van former hookers?"

"No, only one."

Now, arrayed around the living room and adjacent dining room, everyone from both vehicles is asked for impressions. Doug, a dynamic fellow, orchestrates the event. This time, I'm called on, and say, "I'm impressed how nice the ladies are. They appreciate the attention and care. They just need to get rid of those pimps."

The Trafficked Life

Before interviewing the director, Michael, let's introduce four people from his documentary film The Trafficked Life.

Angelica – My mom was a junkie and told me to have sex with men to help her. I came home a hero with money. Then I fell in love with my pimp. He took me away from my mom. Once I started, I either had to continue working or die.

Dana – My pimp told me don't talk to people. He wanted to isolate me so it was easier to sell me for sex. Pimps and johns want young girls. I had to make a certain amount of money each night or I wouldn't eat. I lived in a prison.

Emily – Pimps are mentally and physically abusive. They forced me to have multiple sexual partners. They took me to hotels and houses, and sometimes a lot of people were waiting for me. I had to swallow my pride and become a sexual robot with no feelings

Detective Dustin – Pimps treat young women as a commodity. They dress them up and post their photos online. Selling them is better than selling drugs because once they sell a drug it's gone. A woman is a renewable resource. Just clean them up and they're ready to go again.

* * *

Tom – When women are standing out on a street, like Union Avenue in Bakersfield, why don't they just run away? Or why don't they flag down a cop?

Michael – Many women are afraid to flag down police because they're not jailed until they have a certain amount of misdemeanors. Before that they're just cited and released. Where are they going to go? Pimps have their driver's licenses and cell phones. A lot of women don't realize they're being trafficked. The average starting age is twelve years old. Forty-six percent of those girls know their traffickers. They can be brothers, fathers, husbands.

There's also the Panopticon theory, like a circular jail where one guard can surveil all the prisoners and they don't know if they're being watched. That's how it is on the streets. The women don't know when their pimps are watching. So they often police themselves, and assume they're being watched.

T – I understand that not many pimps are arrested. That's surprising since their criminal behavior seems obvious and very public.

M – Pimps move around a lot. One to four days in a town and they're gone. Bakersfield's on the Interstate 5 corridor going from San Diego and Los Angeles over to San Francisco and back to I-5 to Portland, Seattle, and Vancouver. Highway 58 leads to Las Vegas, the capital of prostitution. Three of the ten worst trafficking cities in the country are in California – L.A., San Diego, and San Francisco.

T – How old are pimps?

M – Twenties and up. But there aren't many old pimps.

T – What races?

M – Across the spectrum, like the girls.

T – How many girls are most pimps managing or enslaving?

M – It's unusual for them to have only one girl, and it's hard for one guy to manage more than ten.

T – While you're filming, have you ever had a confrontation with a pimp?

M – I've never had a confrontation. Pimps are less violent than drug dealers. Many are called "Romeo pimps" and use charm to control the girls. There are also "gorilla pimps" who use force. Some guys like to scare or hurt women.

T – How many times have you been out filming and researching on Union Avenue?

M – Twenty or thirty.

T – Are there any houses of prostitution in Bakersfield?

M – Sure. But I don't know where. That would be off the record, anyway. I imagine some business is done in a few fairly nice hotels around here.

T – Most people don't know much about human trafficking. It's an unpleasant subject.

M – There needs to be more awareness of this problem. I've ridden a bicycle eight hundred miles up and down the Central Valley to raise awareness of human trafficking. In Minnesota five Native American women were kidnapped and murdered as part of a human trafficking operation. Most people haven't heard. This should be a national story and would be if the victims weren't Native Americans.

T – *The Trafficked Life* has already been shown at the Fox Theatre and the Maya Theaters as well as at CSU Bakersfield. How will your film be distributed?

M – We'll enter it in some film festivals. There'll also be some digital options to buy or rent.

T – What's next?

M – I'm working on another project. This time I'm going to give a lot of attention to the johns. Their money's what drives prostitution and human trafficking.

Tips from a Pimp

Don't call me a bad guy. I try to help girls escape problems at home. You don't have to take this, I tell them. You're a beautiful young lady. Come with me. I'll protect and love you. See how much better this is than anything you've ever had.

I know how to take care of girls, usually two to six at a time. Unlike some guys, I'm careful not to overwork my girls. I don't expect fourteen-year olds to have sex twenty to thirty times a day. Once I break them in they usually don't have trouble with ten. Each time they bring me a hundred to three hundred bucks, and I guard the money so the girls don't spend too much on drugs and get paranoid and try to run away. They do that, I have to spank them. But they understand.

I'm the one who protects you from police who love snatching you off the streets, I say. Be careful or they'll lock you up in juvenile hall and then send you straight back to the perverted home you came from. Don't forget Kathi and Jill. They're still in jail. You've only got three choices: hell, fire, or me. And I'll always watch out for you.

I watch as much as I can from safe places and, if possible, I holler when I see or sense trouble. Most of my girls run right back to me when they get out. If they're still young and fresh, and I do mean both, I accept them. Otherwise, I sell them to some guy who's got lower standards.

Pimp Online

I stay out of nice areas where cops look for excuses to stop me. They don't really need excuses, they just turn on the lights. When I want more business I drive around my part of town, looking for girls fifteen, sixteen, or so. If she's hitchhiking, I've got a lead.

"Hey, sweetheart, jump in." I say. "Don't worry. I'm your friend."

I often hear how her dad or stepdad or mother's boyfriend is misbehaving, and her mother either doesn't believe it or is too scared to do anything.

"He tries that shit again, I'll kick his ass," I say. "Whatever it takes to protect you."

I go to motels where they don't ask many questions. When business is good I keep two or three rooms and five or six girls, but there's a lot of turnover, especially if a girl starts smoking too much coke and I have to whip her ass. With my newest girl, I always need to be alone and tell her how and then show her until she's hot and I know she's ready. I used to put them on the street near the motel. But girls standing on streets attract cops who too often convince them to say where they're staying, and then I get busted. I don't want to go back to the hole. I want to be a businessman.

Now I take photos of my girls, in their clothes, in bras and panties, and sometimes naked. Then I post the pictures on websites that handle this stuff, and write words for them about how horny and sweet they are and what they want to do for a man. That way I hook them up privately but always have to be ready for undercover cops posing as johns. There's stress in this business. And sometimes it's hard to figure out what to do about cell phones. I've got to be able to contact the girls about their dates, but having phones lets them call or text whoever they want. I haven't solved that one.

When Dad's a Pervert

My name's Susan. I'm in my twenties and want to tell you this story. My dad was a salesman and weekend preacher. My mom had a home day care center. Dad always had to look perfect on the outside but in truth was an angry and violent man who physically abused our entire family, using his fists or belts to incapacitate us with fear.

He started when I was two, and his invasiveness increased. When I was about seven he said God put me on earth to please men and began taking me to have sex with them. When I was ten we moved to a new church that had men like my dad. The preacher there often had sex with me. Dad said I had to or I'd go to hell. By my teens there were lots of other men. Each one took a piece of me. My happiness and dignity were stolen. I wasn't a person; I was a hollow body for their pleasure.

In high school I began to question if other girls lived that way. Soon, in a motel, I refused to have sex with a man, and my dad beat me with his fists and a belt and pushed my face in the toilet, pulled it out, said never do that again, and then shoved my head back in the toilet. I stopped refusing. I wanted help but didn't know how to get it. I was afraid my dad would kill me. I felt worthless and not good for anything but sex.

I left the church and got help from school counselors and lived out of state one year. No one beat me or used me but I became anorexic and cut myself. I was psychologically tormented but determined never to be trafficked again. I wondered why God hadn't helped me. I was angry at Him for the life He'd given me.

First, I needed a way to support myself but as a minor I couldn't work, get an apartment, or even live in a shelter. I became homeless and a pimp tried to recruit me. I found a part-time job and lived in my old car and then went back to high school and graduated and got a full-time job. A foster family helped me, and I realized religion is not a means of exploiting women.

I attended a support group and overcame huge hurdles. Now I'm free to live life, free to pursue my goals. I'm not unaffected by my history, but I'm not controlled by it. I'm married to a wonderful guy. The Lord rescued and delighted in me.

Getting Girls

I know I'm not pretty but feel I can be if I lose weight. Not many guys in high school ask me out and no one asks more than once. When Johnny, a really cute guy, comes up to me at the mall and tells me I look good, I feel incredible. He invites me to party with some friends of his, two teenage girls like me. They say Johnny's a great guy and really likes me. Sometimes he takes me to dinner and the movies, just us, and I love being with him and know he's the best person I've ever meet. My father never stays with women after babies come, and my mom isn't much help, either, since she smokes crack and drinks. I'm so happy when Johnny asks me to move in with him and his girls. He has two rooms in an old motel in a bad part of town but that doesn't matter.

"You better not," my mother tells me.

"Don't listen," says Johnny. "She's just like my mother."

He makes sure we sleep together once or twice a week, and says he wants me more than the other girls but has to worry about their feelings, too. They're jealous he's buying me clothes and jewelry, but he's already done that for them. I know what they're doing every night they leave the motel. I hope Johnny won't ask me to walk the streets with them.

We move around L.A. every few days until Johnny decides we have to leave town. He says San Francisco, Las Vegas, and Seattle are his favorite cities, and I'll love them, too, and lots of other places he'll take me. I love Johnny more every day. He gives me an engagement ring and hires a guy to tattoo a lion on my back.

"Listen," Johnny says in Stockton, "I'm gonna need some help. Everyone else is working. This'll just be for a little while."

I'm afraid but want to help my man and spend time on the streets and bring johns back to our motel or, for extra, go with them to their homes or motel rooms.

"Don't worry, baby," Johnny says. "Soon we'll be in a beautiful hotel and everyone'll come to you."

I really try to please Johnny but it's hard. He's been telling me to diet, and I have been, but I'm still chubby and guys looking for dates often drive by me and pick up prettier girls. One night I come home, crying.

"What're you doing back so early?" Johnny says. "You gotta earn at least four hundred a night."

"We don't have to. We could get married."

Johnny slaps my face and says, "Get back out there and I don't want to see your fat ass till you've earned your quota."

I stay out all night and come back with less than a hundred dollars.

"I'm sorry, Johnny."

"Where's the rest?"

"That's all I have."

"You spending it on crack again?"

"I told you I just did it a few times."

"No one just does it just a few times." He grabs my arms and squeezes really hard and throws me on the bed and jumps on my stomach, one leg each side of me, and punches me under the left eye. "You're lucky I don't want to damage the merchandise. Tonight I'm selling your ass."

After a couple of weeks with the new guy, I slip out and take a cab to the bus station in Modesto and go back to my mom's.

"You better go get checked up," she says.

I do and find out I'm HIV positive but not giving up. I'm not going to tell anyone. I'm going to lose weight and go find Johnny.

Where's My Daughter?

I started drinking in my mid-teens and for me drinking always meant getting drunk. My girlfriend also drank a lot until we got married and she stopped and started bugging me to do the same. I think we'd still be arguing if she hadn't died of cancer when our daughter, Ellen, was nine. I already had too many responsibilities as a carpenter, father, and husband, and now I was both parents, and anyway I guess guys like me drink more as years go by. I never abused Ellen, not physically or emotionally, and anyone who says I did will get his ass kicked.

Yeah, I know people say my being drunk so much was abusive but it wasn't intentional. I just didn't talk to her as much as I should have, especially when she was about thirteen and guys a few years older started coming around. She was a pretty girl. I wasn't too drunk or preoccupied to understand what was going on.

"Get rid of those guys," I'd tell her. "You're too young to be fooling around."

"Why don't you sober up?"

"Do your damn homework."

I warned a couple of her boyfriends – I guess that's what they were – that I'd deck them if they touched Ellen. I knew they'd already been fooling with her but, really, what could I have done? One weeknight she came in about eleven, a couple of hickeys on her neck, and I jumped up from my chair in front of the TV and grabbed her arm and said, "Cut that out and do like I tell you. From now on you come home right after school and stay home until your grades improve."

She jerked away and went to her bedroom. Next morning she was gone, hadn't bothered to close the window behind her. I called the police who said she'd probably show up soon. They couldn't do anything right away unless I knew where she was. I called the junior high school and explained all I could to the principal and her teachers. I didn't know any of her girl friends since she'd said she was ashamed to bring them home, but through school I got in contact with some who said Ellen had been getting pretty wild.

I wished I'd cared this much earlier. I was devastated. I drove all around our neighborhood and others and her school and stayed on the cops to do something and they promised they were trying. I blew up a recent photo of Ellen, taken by a girl's cell phone at school, and had it made into a flyer I handed out to hundreds of people and posted it all over town.

"Have you seen my little girl?" I asked.

No one had. The cops referred me to a social worker, and she told me, "Ellen may not be in town anymore. They tend to move all over."

"Who are they?"

"Girls being sex trafficked."

"You're saying you think my daughter's a whore."

"Sir, that's not a term we use because it's vulgar and inaccurate. I'm simply telling you that when a thirteen-year-old girl voluntarily disappears I too often learn she's being sex trafficked, like a slave to her pimp."

I didn't say anything. What could I say? I'd never heard of this stuff. Hookers I'd dealt with, years ago and not that many, were grown women and seemed to be working on their own and probably making good money.

"We'll send her flyer to agencies all over the West Coast. They'll put it online. But there are thousands of girls just like yours."

"Thanks, but I don't believe my daughter's in a situation like that. She's probably just living with one of her boyfriends."

Imagine your little girl disappearing. Where was she? I demanded to speak to the detective in charge of cases like this.

"She may be working some of the tracks in cities," he told me. "Some cities, like L.A., have a number of tracks. Even a medium-size city like Fresno has three places."

Every weekend I drove from my home in the Imperial Valley, and cruised the tracks I'd been told about in L.A., Bakersfield, Fresno, San Francisco, and other points on the Highway 99 corridor, passing out my flyers, talking to the ladies, to the girls, in many cases, who were working the streets.

"You lookin' for something?" said a guy in Fresno, strutting toward my window.

"I'm lookin' to blow your ass away if you're pimpin' my daughter," I said, pointing a pistol at his belly. "You seen her?"

"No, man."

"You'll tell me if you do. Right?"

"Right."

"Good, here's a flyer."

I started pulling my gun once or twice a month and got so I wanted to drive down tracks, taking out pimps. I think that would solve the problem but even if it didn't it would still be worthwhile. I used two weeks of vacation time for this search. Ellen's fourteenth birthday passed. Now she'll soon be fifteen. I can't believe no one's seen her flyer or photo online. Haven't some of these people on the streets seen her?

"Sir," said a very young lady in Bakersfield, "maybe she doesn't want you to find her."

"How can that be?"

"She may like her new family more. You better just pray she's alive."

Interview with a Vice Detective

Stephany, a retired vice detective from Los Angeles, currently directs an L.A. organization dedicated to freeing those who've fallen into the bonds of contemporary slavery. She visited Bakersfield to lecture about human sex trafficking, and several days later I called to learn more.

Tom – I'm trying to understand why the girls on the streets, who are in effect slaves, don't call the police or flag them down.

Stephany – The girls don't trust the police. They're often in love with their pimps and don't want to hurt them. They don't see themselves as victims. It's like the Stockholm Syndrome when hostages taken during a bank robbery (in Sweden in 1973) and held a few days began to feel beholden to the hostage takers because they didn't kill them. Some hostages stayed in contact with their captors for years. Prostitutes often stay because they perceive the lack of abuse as kindness. They're also isolated from their families and need a sense of survival.

T – Are pimps usually handsome and charming? They must be in order to control the girls.

S – Many pimps aren't handsome. They go after women with low self-esteem. But sometimes guys with average looks will have beautiful girls. Pimps need psychological tools to control the girls. There's often the physical threat, too. Money drives all this.

T – Even without the girls on the street turning them in, it seems like pimps are out in the open and vulnerable to arrest.

S – I arrested far more johns than pimps. They move around a lot. Sometimes in a single night they'll take their girls from the San Fernando Valley to Hollywood to Compton.

T – District attorneys should be more aggressive and prosecute those guys.

S – DA's are reluctant to prosecute because they don't want a case they can't win. The women usually won't testify.

T – One man who tries to help get women off the streets of Bakersfield told me they use a lot of drugs in order to get through the nightmare of having sex with so many strange and often violent men every night.

S – Every jurisdiction is different. In Los Angeles I saw prostitutes use fewer drugs after the eighties. They're better off sober but many are still tortured, beaten, burned. They're malnourished and have no health care. Some have PTSD. And they're eighteen times more likely to die of murder than other women.

IN FOREIGN LANDS

Abused

I'm Sonia and want you to use my name. In Mexico I had twenty-three brothers and sisters. No, not from the same mother. My dad said he'd lived with eight women before my mom. They had six children together, but he wasn't home much. He'd go away for three or four months, supposedly to work. Sometimes he really was working. He sold fruit and clothes and also opened a restaurant and hotel. He made some money but didn't bring much home because he loved to gamble – poker, dice, horses, cockfighting. He'd bet on anything.

When my dad came home, there was a lot of violence. He hit my mom all the time, and both of them beat the children. They were trying to educate us, like animals. They hit us all over our bodies, using cables, sticks, and wires. Sometimes they'd force us to get on our knees, extend our arms, and hold something heavy in each hand. When I was six-years old he tore off my clothes and abused me. One of my uncles later molested my younger sister, and my dad almost beat him to death.

Sometimes he threatened to kill my mother. Once, when I was about eight, she went away for three days, and I told my dad I'd seen her kissing another man. I wasn't sure I had, and wish I hadn't said anything. He started screaming and hit her in the face so many times you wouldn't have recognized her. After that she took her six kids and one from another family and we moved to Guadalajara. I'd rather not say exactly where we lived. All this could still affect many people. I'll just say we'd moved around Mexico's Costa Alegre between Puerto Vallarta and Manzanillo.

In Guadalajara my mom put my two sisters and me in a convent and told the nuns I should be spanked a lot because I was a naughty girl. My first day there a nun whipped me with a belt and I got spanked just about every day from age eight to eleven. I wet the bed most nights and got more spankings for that. A lot of girls there had the same problem. Sometimes we had to do extra cleaning and sweeping and washing blankets. During naptime I often couldn't sleep, and the

28

nuns sent me to the priest. He sexually molested me on two occasions. He did the same to some of the other girls.

The soap we used to wash blankets was very strong. I was allergic to it and lost most of the skin from my thighs to my feet and developed gangrene. The doctor was going to cut off my legs but Mom came and took me away from the convent and my skin grew back in about a month. I didn't want to return but she made me. I felt helpless. At home she had a new man who also molested me.

When I was eleven my dad took one sister and me to live with him. I was already afraid of men but he gave me presents and taught me how to drive and by the time I was thirteen I thought he loved me when we began sleeping together. He touched me but there was no penetration. I was confused and didn't know what was normal but knew I wasn't happy. Pretty soon my dad, who was fifty-nine, brought his girlfriend to live with us. She was sixteen, a couple years older than I.

At age fifteen I started school and completed fifth and sixth grades in one year. My mom and dad put all their property in my name so someday I could make sure all my brothers and sisters got their share. The law said you either needed to be eighteen or married so Dad forced me to marry a boy of sixteen who smoked and drank and violated me like most men I'd known. I still tried to make it work after we moved to the United States in 1982. I was seventeen. My husband worked for a company that made parachutes in Santa Ana. We had a son but his violence continued so we tried going to churches and marriage counselors. The priests said if we wanted spiritual help and other services we had to get married in the church, which didn't recognize our civil service in Mexico. We had an official ceremony, and two more boys, but my husband continued to be dangerous.

By 1993 I was so desperate I contacted my dad and he said to come live with him. My mother had gone off to live with another man, and one after that, and had five more children. I took my three sons and returned to Mexico. Dad asked for my forgiveness. I agreed and began a new life. I became a businesswoman and sold American clothes on streets and in stores. Fifteen times a year I'd return to the United States to buy clothes to take back to Mexico and sell.

A couple of years later my dad died. I don't have any hate, rancor, or bitterness. He left me in control of his property to share with our family. But he had many debts I worked hard to pay and gave his property to his brothers. I could afford it. In addition to selling clothes I owned a restaurant and invested in a furniture factory. Every week I made several thousand dollars. But Mexico was changing in the mid-nineties as narcotics trafficking and other crimes increased. I drove a big truck like those UPS has and called it my mobile boutique. Criminals robbed me many times. In 1997 three men also assaulted me and I got pregnant. I explained the situation to my three boys, who were between nine and fifteen, and they supported the very difficult decision I made. I wanted the child. She was born in San Jose, California, and unlike my sons this child was mine alone, a gift. It was as if I was born again.

We returned to Mexico but I couldn't bring any clothes or other things to sell. The peso was weaker and the cost of American products kept going up. I needed money, so that December twenty-second I went to Guadalajara to buy clothes. I took my daughter, who was only six-months old. And we were kidnapped. The men threw us in the trunk of a waiting car and drove us somewhere outside the city. When they pulled us out, they began hitting me and I don't remember anything until waking up on the floor of an old house. They had several hidden huts and every day made me sit on men's laps so they could fondle me. They did the same to other women and young girls and even killed some who wouldn't submit. I had to let them sell my body. I'd felt pure, but now I was a slave and a prostitute. These brutal men also smuggled drugs and weapons and even harvested organs.

I was terrified they'd kill my daughter and me. I knew they would. I decided I had to leave my daughter and escape to get help to rescue her. The men caught me and beat and raped me and sent me back to work while I was still healing. When I got a little better, I tried to escape again but they captured me, and this time the beatings were even worse. Still, I waited for another chance to get away. I felt it was either escape or suffer until they decided to kill us. I'd been there three months when I tried again. I didn't have sandals so I wrapped my feet in cardboard, twigs, and leaves, and ran as far as I could, and when I couldn't run I walked harder, longer, faster than I ever had, knowing what they'd do if they caught us, pushing myself, so exhausted and hungry I couldn't continue but forced myself. I had to get to the nearest town. I thought I saw a house. There it was. Then there was another house and another. I'd made it. And I met people who helped me rescue my daughter.

A lot's happened since then. The suffering endured but I began to talk to people about my experiences and established a foundation to help survivors of human trafficking. We're based in Southern California. I travel to give speeches and attend conferences, trying to help women continue to recover. I want all women and children to avoid enslavement and live free and happy lives.

Panty Tree

barren
border
tree
blooms
adolescent
panties

Sold in Chiapas

In Chiapas, the southernmost state in Mexico, many areas are green and tropical and some receive more than a hundred inches of rain a year. It is a fine place to grow crops and easy for absentee landowners to charge poor, often illiterate farmers and their families for working land they've lived on for generations. Exploitation has been particularly severe since forty percent of the people in Chiapas are Indians, and about a third don't speak Spanish. Their malnutrition rate is also highest in Mexico. Starting in 1994 the rights of oppressed have been physically defended by the Zapatista Army of National Liberation (EZLN) which revolted against the Mexican Army as well as paramilitaries paid by landowners. The EZLN commands many villages and much indigenous support, and the region remains volatile.

In this environment, about two years before the revolt, Lourdes lived in a shack on a farm with her parents and so many brothers and sisters she never counted. Her father, an Indian who spoke little Spanish, was unhappy in the fields and often drunk at home. Facing an eternity of many obligations and few assets, he one evening resolved to sell twelve-year-old Lourdes to a coyote who promised he'd take the girl to work in the fields near Los Angeles and she'd earn more in a month than her father in a year.

If Lourdes' father believed he was somehow blueprinting a better life for his daughter, he was incorrect: she was first taken to Tijuana where every night her slender body was mauled by customers who paid the coyote. In a few months he decided business would be better to the North, so he first smuggled Lourdes and several other girls somewhere near San Diego and then to a Los Angeles suburb. In both places Lourdes lived in a house with about twenty other slaves. For four years the work load was heavy, sometimes more than ten rowdy men a night. Twice Lourdes got pregnant. She lost the first because of general trauma. The second time the coyote kicked her in the stomach.

Lourdes ran away at age sixteen, hitchhiking north into then up the Central Valley, continuing her original profession but, in revulsion, dreaming of something else. She met other young women who told her, "You don't have to do this. Try the fields." For several years she picked crops from Bakersfield to Delano to Tulare to Fresno to Sacramento and back, and on a Saturday night in the capital city Lourdes met a guy in a bar and was thrilled he treated her respectfully. A day later she decided he loved her, and in one week they were married. Now Lourdes stays home in Bakersfield, caring for her two small children. She has not contacted her father nor does she plan to.

Wanted: Little Girls

Jeff is in a Cambodian house, portraying a man in search of little girls. He's learned they're being held in several pens dispersed in a town, and arranges to meet the trafficker who brags he has many for rent. What kind do you want? About this tall? He extends a hand. Too big? He lowers his hand. How about that? Maybe eight-years old, nice and fresh. Some are young as five. Jeff pays to meet a girl privately and sees blank and lifeless eyes. The girl flinches. He motions no, he's not here for that, and teaches her to play rock breaks scissors cut paper wraps rock. She relaxes a little. He'd like to get her and others out of this life but police make about thirty dollars a month and two men in uniforms visit, more eager to accept bribes than liberate children.

Jeff has to move on. During his next investigation he receives a tip that an American in his late sixties is imprisoning underage girls in his bar and restaurant. Jeff enters and orders orange juice. The men exchange first names and chat about sports, tropical scenery, and local poverty.

"I'm looking for a girl," Jeff says.

"Got three you'd love."

"Where are they?"

"Takes a little time for a personal showing," Todd says. "Tomorrow, maybe I can play a little video, if you like."

"Sure."

Jeff returns for more orange juice and says, "Where's the action?"

"Right here." Todd sets a small TV on the bar, plugs in a VCR tape, and turns on the machine. "They're thirteen, fourteen, and fifteen, and I trained 'em myself. Look."

On screen he individually kisses and fondles the girls before shoving their faces onto his penis and occasionally slaps or spanks them before forcing himself inside, and in one scene rolls on the bed with all three.

"Come here, Tina," he says to a slender woman in her thirties. "This is my girlfriend from Vietnam. She gets girls for me and my customers."

"Very easy," she says.

"Nice," Jeff says. "How'd they get here?"

"Tina promises parents we'll give their daughters good jobs, nice places to stay, and better money than they earn at home."

"Love to meet 'em," Jeff says.

"Come back tomorrow."

The next day the bar owner says, "Want something stronger then orange juice for the show?

"No, I'm fine."

Tina leads the girls out and speaks to them in Vietnamese. They're dressed in hot pants and halter tops and remove the tops and begin to dance to rock music projected through speakers mounted on the wall behind the bar. After about ten minutes Todd motions for the girls to come and say hello to Jeff. They smile when he introduces himself.

"Show Jeff a little more." Tina translates a message that turns their eyes to the floor. "Take them up to their room, sweetheart."

She motions to the stairs and follows them to the second floor.

"Maybe I could visit one of them in their room sometime," Jeff says.

"Just send the other two out. Unless you want to pay for all three."

"Love to, if they're still here."

Todd smiles. He keeps the girls locked in a room with one barred window."

Promising he'll be back soon, Jeff leaves and takes his undercover recording equipment to Cambodian police. This time they cooperate, using Jeff's video to get an arrest warrant. Meanwhile, two of the three girls have pried the door open late at night and escaped. Todd sends Tina back to Vietnam. She returns with another girl who's with the remaining captive when police raid the bar and arrest the couple. Todd and Tina spend a few days in jail before he pays the judge twenty-five thousand dollars to be released.

Cambodian police and Jeff learn that Todd had unlawfully fled Oregon after being charged with child abuse and molestation of his niece. Jeff contacts Interpol. Again, Cambodian police arrest Todd, but this time drive straight to the airport. U.S. Marshals accompany him back to Oregon where he's serving twenty-three years.

Interview with Jeff

Tom – What laws were you and the Cambodian police dealing with?

Jeff – We used the existing warrant from Oregon and the extradition treaty between Cambodia and the United States. We also could have used the Trafficking Victims Protection Act of 2000 which states that a U.S. citizen who traffics or exploits a minor can be extradited to the United States from anywhere in the world.

T – That's a good law, but it seems like human trafficking is growing fast.

J – I don't know if trafficking is growing fast. People are more aware now and there are more prosecutions.

T – How did you get involved in this battle?

J – Starting in 1984 I was a police officer in Kansas City. I worked narcotics and vice, but in the late eighties and early nineties most people, including the police, didn't consider involuntary prostitution to be trafficking. People believed it was like domestic violence. The perception was that the girls and women could leave if they wanted. We now understand that's often not the case.

I was the chief of police in Butler, Missouri for five years before retiring in 2006. That year I was hired by the Internal Justice Mission. A majority of our work is overseas. We try to help change the justice system in countries, working with the police and courts, to see how the laws can be improved. I've worked in twenty-two countries to date.

T – What are some of the countries?

J – In Southeast Asia – Cambodia, Thailand, Laos, Vietnam; in South Asia – India, Bangladesh, and Nepal; in Africa – Kenya, Uganda, Rwanda, Zambia, and Ethopia; in Europe – Russian, Poland, Amsterdam, Italy, France, and Germany. Among others.

T – The United States being one of them.

J – That's right.

Young Stuff

Settle down, people, I'm John Billingsley the actor not my perverted character Malcolm Eddery in *Trade of Innocents*. It's all make-believe. Well, it's actually quite real for the victims and their abusers and based on sources we trust. That's why it upsets me playing a man who thinks: this is an outrageous inconvenience; I finally convince my wife I have business in Southeast Asia, pay thousands to fly to Cambodia, and the lousy pimp offers me a girl twelve years old and claims she's a virgin; like hell; I know she's been sewn up; no way four thousand, not three either, two thousand max; and damn soon I want two virgins no more than seven; I'll pay fifty grand for a month; first, show them porn so they'll know how to please me; I'll give them plenty of ice cream and clean them up afterward because they're going to be messy.

Born into Brothels

We are boys and girls, millions *Born into Brothels* in India and excited to be in a documentary and pleased filmmakers want us to study photography now and learn to feel positive and get into good schools or we'll be doomed to continue living where prostitutes, pimps, and thieves don't like pictures taken and scream you worthless little cunt, I'll beat you son of bitch, you think you're saintly but you're twice as bad.

We hate rooms with curtains on rods dividing us from strange men who screw our mothers then get drunk and shout they won't pay for alcohol. Fathers also demand free booze and beat mothers who buy drugs instead of giving money. Sometimes it's worse and the pimp'll set our mothers on fire because everyone knows police do nothing.

Where are authorities when some children are chained at home, visible to passersby, while mothers walk the streets? Where are doctors when a woman loses six sons and a husband and then tries to kill herself? Where is social support when a great grandmother's a former whore, a grandmother's a former whore, and a mother is a whore? Who can stop parents and other relatives forcing children into that? Who consoles a boy already convinced life must be painful and sad? Who treats or prosecutes a father sitting out front in the street, smoking hashish all day? Who is responsible for picking up rotting garbage all around?

We're children and can't resolve problems but take beautiful pictures and see our work exhibited in a gallery and written about in newspapers before filmmakers again stress we're doomed unless we get into good schools which usually don't take children of prostitutes, pimps, and thieves. We better go to boarding schools or we'll just be returning every afternoon to the red light district. To escape we need documents the filmmakers have filled out and pasted in our photos. We must also provide medical proof we don't have HIV already consuming many mothers.

Some of us are interviewed by a strict school director who says if accepted we must make a ten-year commitment and vow not to leave campus except for two or three ten-day vacations yearly. If we live and study like that we can be doctors, engineers, anything. Several of us are selected to attend good schools. We then learn one of us returns home, another's father says no go, another's mother forces withdrawal, a girl quits, a kid runs away, another's mother denies the chance to get out, and one kid is in school and doing well.

Employment Agent

I traveled to remote and impoverished villages in India and saw mothers broken by ten children and life in hovels. Food was scarce and medical care either horrific or nonexistent. I was proud to give their daughters a chance to earn decent wages cleaning houses and working in factories. I offered encouragement and transportation to big cities where agents promised new lives.

I trusted those guys and didn't know some girls were imprisoned in homes of people who demanded eighteen hours work a day and abused them. I also had no idea some girls young as twelve were forced into prostitution, so it's outrageous authorities charge I sometimes freely used their services before saying farewell. I simply delivered the girls to agents at train stations. I shouldn't be in jail now. Most of my colleagues are free.

Iraqi Woman

When I was twelve my father, a failed shopkeeper, received money and jewelry from an old man of forty who took me as his wife. The first time alone was a nightmare like every time until another old man, who paid my husband, took me to live in a large old house, surrounded by battered walls, with several of his "women," four girls about my age. Three said they'd been kidnapped, and the other, like me, was a salable wife. The new old man grabbed whichever he wanted for a night but soon focused on renting us to men who did whatever and snickered about the superiority of young stuff.

We moved to cities and towns around Iraq wherever the old man heard business was good. He always told us be nice to men or he'd slap us. I wanted to kill him and might have but I was arrested for prostitution and in jail several months. I didn't want to go home but had nowhere else. When I arrived my family called me filth and said get away before I shamed them more. I don't have a real home but found a little better old man who appreciates money I earn and may let me learn to read.

House Arrest

A Filipina says she's sad three teenagers were kidnapped in Cleveland a decade ago and caged prior to endless abuse but doesn't understand how the pervert prevented them from killing him or escaping or making noise to alert neighbors. She cites her first job as a maid. Her employer demanded she join his wife for a hot threesome. When she shouted I'm not a prostitute, he locked her in a room with two other maids. Next morning she assumed the man was at work, pulled the mattress off a bed, took apart the bed frame, and readied a metal spear.

PROSTITUTION

LATIN FLAVOR

Prostitutes in Madrid

My first evening in Madrid I strolled from my hotel a hundred yards to Gran Via, the most celebrated street in Spain and frequent scene from movies highlighting its ornate old buildings and statues that hold up balconies bordered by iron railings. After waiting for frenetic traffic to stop at a red light, many people and I crossed Gran Via, and I headed straight to what I considered a plaza but, technically, is very wide Calle Montera, a street with no vehicles, unless they belong to the police, and that's lined by shops and restaurants and sidewalk cafes. On the right side of the street every several yards or so, frequently next to rather skinny trees, stood young women wearing hot pants, halter tops, and lots of makeup and lipstick. On the left side, interspersed with diners and shoppers, several muscular, blue-uniformed members of the Madrid Police leisurely patrolled.

The second or third working lady I passed said in English, "Let's go."

Without looking at her, I continued walking. A few seconds later a beautiful blonde said in Spanish, "Come here."

I complied, and we continued in Spanish. "Come with me."

"Sorry, but I can't," I said.

"Come on."

"Really, I can't. I'm going to a play. But out of curiosity, how much?"

"Twenty-five euros for twenty minutes," she said. That's about forty dollars.

"Where do you go?"

"To an apartment very near here."

"Do you live there?"

"No, there are ten bedrooms we use." She stepped close, softly held my arm, then leaned into me.

"What about the police?"

"No problem."

"Where are you from?"

"Romania," she said.

47

"You speak Spanish well. But I've got to go."

"You could come with me first, then go to the play."

"Adios."

"You're bad."

I ignored a few more propositions walking down Calle Montera en route to adjacent Plaza Puerto del Sol where hordes of young people protest political issues and sell watches, clothes, and art. And then I took a cab to the Matadero, once a massive series of slaughter-houses, and watched *Incrementum*, a humorous play about six women angry with their "jefe del departmento," the boss. These stunning and dynamic young actresses, I felt, must have begun life under more congenial circumstances than the prostitutes.

The following day I began talking to taxi drivers, hotel workers, waiters, and others about my experiences with the ladies on the street. They usually responded that most of the women on Calle Montera are from Romania though some come from Bulgaria and Slovenia and elsewhere in the European Union, which allows citizens from member nations easy movement for residence and work. Legally or illegally overcoming documentary difficulties are many women from Russia, Africa, and South America.

"I'm surprised the police don't do anything," I told one taxi driver.

"The police, like many in Spain, believe that prostitution is a way of living, and the women sell their bodies to survive," he said.

"Is there ever any trouble?"

"Yes. The girls look for foreigners. They say twenty-five euros but they're not going upstairs for that. When they're talking to men, their chulos (pimps) are watching, and they'll follow them and rob them if they can. Watch out for those guys. Sometimes, when the girl and the guy are in her room, she'll slip him a pill with a kiss that knocks him out and when he wakes up his money, credit cards, and passport are gone."

I asked another taxi driver, "Does that really happen?"

"It can happen, but not much. There are much tougher areas than Calle Montera. One is called Villaverde. Women are on the street twenty-four hours a day."

It was around ten a.m. when I said, "Let's go."

In about fifteen minutes we arrived in an industrial area dominated by warehouses and heavy equipment, and cruised a couple of streets before seeing the first lady, a statuesque brunette, about twenty-five, clad in a long stylish white dress and high heels and who could decorate the covers of fashion magazines. I powered my window down and motioned for her to come to the taxi.

"Hola, cómo estás?"

"Why are you speaking Spanish?" she said in fluent English.

"I want to practice. Where are you from?"

"Romania."

"And how much?"

"One hundred euros for one hour," a hundred sixty bucks.

"Where would we go?

"There's a hotel near here," she said.

"Muchas gracias," I said, and powered the window up. Gracefully she turned and walked back to sparse shade under a scraggly tree.

We moved on and within a couple of minutes passed several more women, most wearing miniskirts or hot pants and halter tops. I motioned for the taxi driver to pull over, and summoned an attractive but somewhat chunky lady in her mid-thirties. Undaunted by formidable competition, she also wanted a hundred euros for sixty minutes labor.

"Are you from Romania?"

"Bulgaria."

"Where would we go?"

"To my house," she said.

I thanked her, and the taxi driver moved on and said, "These girls also sell a lot of drugs: marijuana, cocaine, ecstasy. There's a good chance guys she takes home have problems with her chulo. And they don't change the sheets afterward in the houses."

"Aren't there any girls from Spain on the streets?" I asked.

"Almost none. Spanish women are in nice clubs or available by telephone. They get a hundred to three hundred euros per hour, plus cab fare."

These experiences were enlightening but satisfied my desire for information about the subject. That night about midnight, after watching an Israeli movie with Spanish subtitles and eating a late buffet dinner, I crossed Gran Via and wearily walked along a boulevard still relatively busy with traffic and pedestrians. Suddenly, a pretty woman appeared at my left side. I was holding my omnipresent notebook in my right hand.

"I love you," she said in perfect English. "Come to my apartment and sleep with me."

"No thanks."

"Why not?"

"Where are you from?"

"Ghana."

I walked a little faster but she kept bombarding me with offers and started bumping me and then seized my left arm with both of hers, sending a shock from my heart to brain, and I ripped my arm free and shoved her and spun around and saw a large young man, who'd clearly been closing in, abruptly change directions and walk fast down the sidewalk, looking straight ahead.

"Don't push me," she said.

"Do you speak Spanish?"

"Yes."

"No mas."

Colombian Dalliance

Look, we were just relaxing at a hotel bar in Cartagena. Even secret service agents and soldiers have a right to relax. Indeed, we had a duty to unwind because if uptight we might not be as attuned to potential danger to President Obama, who was going to arrive in a few days.

What's the big deal about twenty of us taking women back to rooms? I guarantee my woman wasn't a prostitute. She didn't ask for money. She couldn't have been anything bad. I think she said she was teacher or maybe a secretary.

I'm shocked some agents said they were with prostitutes. They didn't look like pros. They were just hot lookin' Colombian babes. Know what I mean? Frankly, I feel sorry for guys who couldn't find regular women. Agents must maintain pride in appearance and personality and know they can get it without paying and consorting with dangerous criminals. I feel good about what I did but my wife's pretty upset.

Central American Nights

On a hot and sticky late afternoon I walk along Lake Managua, looking at water gray and dead as downtown rubble left by the 1972 earthquake. I assume lucky fish have died and those left are contaminated. Sweating and tired I turn and walk to the nearby Piano Bar and begin ordering two Victoria beers at once and drinking fast. The bartender pleases me with news that Howard Hughes also stayed at the Hotel Intercontinental. But Hughes undoubtedly lived in the penthouse while I dislike my small, old room and don't want to go back. I don't have to. I drink at the Piano Bar until recorded music booms across the street by the hotel pool.

Two young black women are walking that way, too. They look approachable, and in Spanish I say, "Ladies, would you like to join me at the cabaña?"

"Sí," they say.

"Where are you from?"

"Bluefields, on the Caribbean," says the older sister. The younger is pretty but quiet.

"What are you doing in Managua?"

"We're working. There aren't many jobs in Bluefields."

The ladies order mixed drinks and I continue pounding Victorias, though now I order one at a time. Soon a white man in his thirties, my age, comes to our table and asks if he can join us. Of course he can.

"Where're you from?" I ask.

"Czechoslovakia," he says. He's working for the Sandinistas and helping restore projects the Contras have been blowing up.

I ask the younger sister, Elizabeth, to dance. She moves much better than I but that doesn't matter. I lean over and kiss her cheek and neck and say, "Let's go to my room." We agree on a price, the Cordoba equivalent of forty dollars, and return to our table. Elizabeth's sister and the Czech have already departed.

"Let's have some more drinks first," I say.

A couple hours later we enter the hotel. A suspicious bellhop waves a no-no index finger. We walk out and watch the man and the desk clerk until surveillance lapses then we run to the elevator. In a room almost as muggy as outside I think about AIDS and indignity and decide not to proceed. Instead, we chat a couple of hours before saying goodnight.

It's four a.m. and when my wakeup call comes at six I wish I hadn't drunk so much. I almost heave during the short flight to San Jose. At the Gran Hotel Costa Rica I check in and ask them to send up two helpings of bacon, eggs, rice, beans, and orange juice. The food helps my stomach but not my head. I undress and lie on the bed. After awhile I'm asleep. That afternoon someone coming in awakens me and I struggle up and rush to the door, meeting an old maid who stops, turns around, and walks out fast.

By late afternoon I'm able to get up and consider calling room service for dinner but need to get out. I'm still ill but know how to fix that. I walk downstairs and ask a bellhop, "Where's the best bar in town?"

"Key Largo, señor, excelente, and not far."

Out of the taxi I step and look into darkening clouds that frame a three-story gothic mansion like the eerie place where Humphrey Bogart and Edward G. Robinson fired pistols at each other. Inside, the lights are bright for a bar and I wish they weren't. I'm pale and puffy under the eyes so only glance at several young ladies seated around the large rectangular bar. I order tequila and orange juice and soon begin to feel better, especially when a lovely black-haired lady smiles at me. I hope she did. The bell hop will get a tip for that. Soon, as my next drink arrives, a delightful brunette, seated across the bar, points red lips at me, and I think no way I look good enough for that to happen twice.

The brunette gets up, glides around the bar, and sits on the next stool.

"I'd like to, but don't do that anymore."

"What?"

"You should go to school, get a job, not this. Would you like a drink?"

She does.

"I don't have money to go to school. And there aren't many

53

good jobs."

"There must be some."

I feel more righteous and expert each drink but the place is filling up and the lady smiles and says, "I have to go," and moves to another man.

Filling the vacancy, a blonde sits beside me.

"Why are you doing this?"

"I have to."

"You don't like it, do you?"

"I'll give you a good time."

"I can't."

"Why?"

"Same reason you'll stop someday."

"Rich Americans don't understand."

"I'm not rich."

"Compared to me."

"Señor," I say to the bartender. "Will that TV get the Sugar Ray Leonard-Tommy Hearns fight tonight?"

"Sí, we have a satellite."

"Please watch the fight with me? It'll be great, like their first fight."

"Fifty dollars for the fight. Then the rest."

"You're pretty expensive."

"I'm worth it."

La Cubana

Back at the Havana hotel I took my second shower of the day before descending to the pool where I sat in the shade slurping cold Heinekens but was sweating in a tropical sauna that compelled a retreat to my room for a nap and another shower – three was my daily average this trip. I wanted to be fresh that night for the vaunted Tropicana nightclub selling tickets for about thirty bucks, a sizable sum for a socialist paradise in the early nineties. Most revelers were tourists, with a few party functionaries, in an outdoor facility fashioned to resemble an exotic island. As a Californian, I thought the club had a Pacific feel but decided in this region decorators must have been thinking Caribbean.

I found the final seat at the bar and started knocking down cold Heinekens, the only available beer less powerful than local wine-like Hatuey. A comely young lady of African descent sat on the stool next to me. After polite introductions in Spanish, I asked, "Would you like a drink?"

"Gracias."

"I'm a teacher. What do you do?"

"I'm a secretary."

"For the government?"

"Everything's for the government."

"Sí, that's what I've always heard."

"I like the way you speak Spanish," she said, arousing me with her smile.

"It's a romantic language."

I was already planning a hot Cuban dalliance and, if diplomatically feasible, bringing her to California for a few weeks. Alas, even in this alcohol-induced state of merriment, I soon noted she'd begun glancing into my wallet each time I paid the bartender.

"Hay algo de interes en mi cartera?" I asked. ("Is there something of interest in my wallet?")

"Oh, no," she said.

55

In a little while she urged me to buy a huge, twelve-dollar Cuban cigar for her male friend, perhaps her agent, who'd just appeared. I declined, and the woman said, "You don't buy anything for anyone."

I should've quit drinking and looked for another seat. Instead I soothed myself with more bitter beers, and enjoyed a succession of singers and dancers and acrobats accompanied by powerful live music that seemed a fusion of Bob Marley and Desi Arnaz. After the show, having established that I was a worldly man and not to be trifled with, I invited the working lady to join me on the rounds of Havana nightlife. We circulated until bars closed at five a.m. In the hotel lobby, vigilant employees suggested I send her home.

Too early that morning, around noon, I received a call from a female friend of the lady. She wanted to meet me. I was honored but declined since I had to arrange a taxi to take me to Hemingway's house.

The Pink Zone

Without complication Buck paid the hundred-fifty peso cover charge and entered a place full of smoke and energy and young adults. He stood awhile and watched the band. The keyboard player sang like Jim Morrison as the group hammered "Twentieth Century Fox."

"Buenas noches, señor," said a handsome young man. "Do you like women?"

"Of course."

"Please come and sit with my two friends. They're lonely."

One was fair and blond and the other had brown skin and long black hair. Both were stunning.

"Hola, I'm Buck."

"I'm Marisela."

"And I'm Juana," said the blonde.

"I'm Jesus, and I'll talk to you later."

"Would you like a drink?" Buck asked.

"Dos cervezas," said Marisela.

"Tres, por favor," Buck told the waitress in a mini skirt.

"Are you from here?" he asked the two ladies.

"I'm from a small town in Michoacán," Marisela said.

"I'm from Monterrey," said Juana.

"A vacation?"

"We're here to work," said Marisela.

"What do you do?"

"We work in a factory," Marisela said.

"What do you make?"

"Dresses," said Marisela. "And you?"

"I'm a farmer."

"Do you have a big farm?" she asked.

"So so."

The beers arrived. One was normal size but two tiny bottles looked like perfume samples.

"Two hundred fifty pesos, señor," said the waitress.

"Really?"

"Sí, one hundred for each of the ladies and fifty for you."

"Gracias," said Buck. He leaned back and sipped his beer. "This place is expensive."

"One has to pay for quality," said Marisela.

"Here's some now. 'Love Me Two Times', baby…" Would you like to dance, Juana?"

On the crowded floor, amid flashing colored lights, Buck watched the long-haired keyboard player pound away and sing, and he raised both hands, snapping fingers and shaking his rear, and she moved gracefully as they danced to several Doors' classics. Afterward, Buck put his arm around Juana and escorted her back to the table. "Mexico's my new home," he said.

Looking earnestly at him, Marisela leaned over and put both hands on his thigh and in English asked: "Do you want to fuuck both of us?"

"What? Of course not."

"Let's go," Marisela told Juana.

"Don't go, Juana."

"He's cheap," Marisela said, standing.

"Okay. How much?"

"Five hundred pesos, but just for me," said Juana.

"For how long?"

"One hour."

"Fine."

Marisela walked to another table, whispered something to a man who nodded, and she sat down.

Three more beers arrived.

"I didn't order these," Buck said.

"When you're with ladies, the drinks always come," said the waitress.

"Okay, but now, just two."

"I'll drink these two," Juana said, collaring the little ones.

Buck paid.

"Are you angry?"

"No, I just thought…"

"I have three children in Monterrey."

"Monterrey's a big city. Isn't there a lot of work there?"

"Not good work."

"But you could study in college."

"No, I couldn't. My father made me quit school when I was ten."

"Why?"

"To take care of my brothers and sisters."

"You could do regular work during the day and study at night."

"I'm working tonight. Are you going to pay me?"

"Oh. Sí."

"Let's go, then."

As they left, the keyboard player wailed: "Come on baby, 'Light My Fire.'"

When they arrived at the front of the hotel, the doorman said, "Señor, I believe you checked in alone. I'm sorry. No guests in your room."

Buck put his arm around Juana and guided her toward the elevator some thirty meters away. When they arrived, four uniformed hotel employees were waiting.

"Sorry, señor," said one of them. "Only hotel guests in the rooms."

"She's a guest."

"Is she registered?"

"Of course."

"Your name?"

"Buck Wilson."

He pulled out an electronic device and softly spoke into it. Within thirty seconds he told Buck, "Sorry, señor."

"Don't worry," Juana said. "I know a very economical hotel."

In their entirely clean room, about ten minutes from La Zona Rosa, Juana took off her dress and stood in her underwear and bra, looking at Buck. "What do you want?"

"I just want, uh…"

Juana stepped up to Buck and they embraced and he tried to kiss her lips but she pulled away, and with his left hand he touched her face and eased it toward him and kissed her until she jerked away and said: "No."

"Why not?"

She didn't reply.

Buck enveloped her and they bounded into bed and he proceeded with the passion and endurance of a man long-deprived, rested only minutes before starting again, and despaired when she said, "Señor, my god, please stop."

He exhaled and collapsed. She put both hands on his chest and pushed him aside. In a little while, as they looked at the ceiling, she said "That's one hour, señor."

He reached for his pants. "Here's five hundred pesos."

"Gracias."

"A little more."

She sighed, and said: "Fine."

An hour and twenty minutes later she was standing naked and using a bar of bathroom soap to write on the large mirror opposite the foot of the bed. Her equation read: $500 \times 1\ 1/3 = 500 \times 4/3 = 2000/3 = 700$ pesos.

"Would you like to go to the pyramids tomorrow?"

"I work tomorrow."

"Why don't you come with me in the morning?"

"You're a silly man," she said, and walked out.

As Buck left the economical hotel he passed a room exposed by an open door. Juana and Marisela, and two other women, and their friend Jesus were lounging on two beds.

"Buenas noches," said Buck.

They did not reply.

Melina on Sunday

I've been working the streets several years and don't like being there but can't get away long. If I could I'd live like this lady I'm watching in the movie *Never on Sunday.* She's the happiest hooker I've seen, smiling as she runs toward the sea, through lines of adoring dockworkers, and jumps off the pier and all the men follow and tread water as they ask about her schedule. She'll let them know. She's independent.

When two sailors approach in a bar, she chooses the low bidder, telling the other she doesn't like him.

"I don't make it a condition that you like me," he says.

"I make it a condition," she tells him, escorting the other out of the bar.

She refuses to work Sundays, and hosts open house for special friends. My boyfriend would beat me if he caught me watching something like this. He beats me for less. I'll just keep the door locked and turn the TV off when I hear his hand on the door. He's got my phone but I've secretly got my friend's and go online to look up this movie. The star is Melina Mercouri in 1960. There's also a new American guy in Greece who already loves her and doesn't change even after he finds out about her work. He's director Jules Dassin who several years later will become her husband, and I'm sure he'll get her in the film, too.

Jules is a scholar, loves Aristotle and those guys, and is impressed Melina speaks French, Italian, Greek, Spanish, and English, and asks, "Where did you learn all those languages?"

"In bed," she says.

That sounds good on screen but makes me cringe because what I usually learn in bed is that too many men smell bad and act worse.

I really like Melina, who's a pretty lady with long golden brown hair. She tells Jules there's a man in that car called No Face who owns a street of apartments and all the girls live there and fear him. Not Melina. She's a free agent. I'd love to be like her and have my own place and host a house full of adoring men except I don't know any of those.

Jules asks a local man if this "vice king," who I'd call a pimp, might hurt Melina.

"She has too many friends," he says. "We'd kill him."

I love my boyfriend but there are plenty of times I'd like someone to kill his brutal ass. I wish I could live in Greece near Melina. She should listen when Jules tells her "a whore can't be happy" and tries to transform her with education. That's the best way. Every day I pay for quitting school in ninth grade. Jules is right telling a man that prostitution "is revenge against all women."

No Face starts warning the other hookers to stay away from Melina. One of the girls then complains to Jules that No Face charges too much – a hundred eighty drachmas – and if a girl moves out "he makes it so she can't find another place." He won't make maximum money as long as Melina's influencing the girls so he approaches Jules and says, "We both want Melina to retire."

A dark, handsome Italian becomes one of Melina's clients and they make love all the time, and when he talks about emotions, she says it's forbidden to say "love" but then embraces him for more. I need some johns like this guy. I like Jules, too, but he's kind of short and Melina keeps telling him he's got a big nose.

Jules is so determined. He convinces Melina she isn't happy with her work, even though she claims she is, and gets her to commit two weeks learning about culture. He spends a lot of money loading her apartment with books, a piano, a record player for classical music, and a wicked portrait of Picasso's wife to replace the picture of a soccer team Jules takes down. Judging by that image, I decide Picasso should've been a pimp.

A week later Melina tells a man she isn't having as much fun but her new life is better. She may fool him but not herself. She's sad and looks at the soccer picture and puts away the serious classical stuff and plays "Never on Sunday," a beautiful song she sings as she reclines on her bed and smokes. She's soon excited when a naval vessel, loaded with men, blows its horn coming into port after weeks at sea.

In another part of town one of the girls catches Jules talking to No Face and hurries to tell Melina. Jules shows up at her apartment and the girl, who's husky but sexy, accuses him of having dirty money in his pocket. When Melina discovers that's true she goes wild, throwing books and pictures and takes a broom to a glass-covered photo and breaks a record on the poor man's head. I'd do the same.

As sailors cheer below, Melina and the other girls throw furniture out their windows. In jail Melina tells No Face's lawyer a hundred eighty drachmas are too much. Okay, one-seventy. No, eighty, she demands. One-sixty, then. No. How about one-twenty? Ninety. That's what they agree on, and Melina rides in triumph to the bar where Jules, desperate to impress her, chugs liquor and dances not too bad for a white man, and tells her he's wanted her from the start and still wants to save her. Melina's not mad anymore. The handsome Italian sweeps her into his arms and carries me away.

ILLEGAL

Brief History of a John

I know John. So do you. Everyone does. He's a great guy. We were drinking coffee in a restaurant the other day, and I said, "Best I've ever had were in Vegas."

"Well, you'd know about that."

"What? You tellin' me you've never paid."

"Only a few times, probably less than ten."

"Love to hear about those experiences."

"You won't tell anyone?"

"Of course not."

This is what John said. I know because I recorded him:

I was raised in Sacramento, and as soon as guys in my junior year started getting our licenses we cruised downtown to 4th and S Streets. When you're sixteen it's exciting to be out late at night and drive by nice looking women who, many times a day, I guess, did what most of us never had. These were mostly black women, too, and we hadn't really known any. There were just three blacks in my high school in the late sixties. A few of us went down together, usually in my car, every weekend for about a month. We didn't stay long. One night I pulled over and rolled down my window and asked, "How much for a quick one?"

"Twenty," one said, leaning into my window. Three of her friends stood around her.

"How about ten?"

"You're just little boys jivin'," she said.

"No, we're serious," said Jack from the back seat.

"It's cold tonight," I said. "You guys must be freezing."

"Unless some money starts comin' out of this window, this conversation is over."

I really didn't want to do anything. They seemed kind of tough. But Jack hopped out and handed one of the other ladies a twenty, and she led him behind some heavy bushes that lined S Street, I think. Jack returned about ten minutes later.

"How was it?" I asked.

"Okay," he said, and we never mentioned it again.

Quite a few guys in our class went to Mustang Ranch outside Reno. That was a better setup: everything legal and no danger on the streets. Four of us drove up Interstate 80 on a Saturday afternoon. Once we got close we got our beers out of the trunk and drank a few each since we were pretty nervous. The ladies came out and lined up, smiling at us like we were kids, which we were, compared to them. I picked a short blonde with big tits. She took me back to a room and asked what I wanted. I paid, and she washed my cock. That was years before they required rubbers. Rubbers would've been unthinkable in those days. I got pretty excited, even before she undressed, and tried to kiss her but she wouldn't let me, and now I'm glad she didn't. Once we got started I really enjoyed it, the two minutes it lasted. I remember the climax quite well. But I wish my first time had been for real, not with a hooker.

My first year in college I met a girl I dated a few years, and we got married when I was twenty-two. I guess I wasn't ready. After a couple of years I found I wanted to have sex with other women, but I'm really not a great socializer or hustler. I got so I started masturbating a few times a week. My wife figured that out and was mad as hell. I don't know why she minded, except we were having sex less and less. I told her to masturbate, too. That didn't go over well.

A friend told me about a massage parlor near Sacramento City College. I didn't even bother with the massage. The woman I got – there wasn't a selection like at Mustang Ranch – was kind of chunky and not as attractive as my wife, but she was new, and that made it pretty good. I was learning what torments me more every year: not every man is made to have sex with the same woman for fifty or sixty years. I know many women are the same or at least similar. People can moralize about monogamy and being faithful all they want, but for lots of people – a quarter, a third, a half, whatever – it's unrealistic. A friend of mine sometimes says, "No man is any more faithful than his last good opportunity." That was certainly true for me. If I'd had the options of rock stars and professional athletes, I'd have done hundreds of women.

My wife left me a couple of years later. She was having an affair with another guy. I was devastated, but I'm not sure why. Our marriage needed to end. But the end's going to be painful because husbands and wives usually have a lot of affection for each other even if they've lost the passion. Frankly, I was horny to the point I was miserable. I went to bars and nightclubs quite a bit and had some one-nighters and short relationships but nothing substantial. In the early eighties I went to Las Vegas once or twice a year and met some girls there, but they were pretty hardnosed. In my hotel room, while my lady for that night used the bathroom, I hid my wallet between the mattresses. After we finished and I used the bathroom, she was gone. I thought, at least I've got my wallet, but she'd taken it. I guess they always check the mattresses.

I got married again a couple years later. Listen, as I've said, I'm no swinger but after a while I just had to go to bed with someone else. I drove to Ensenada with a few buddies for deep sea fishing. After a few days there, and not getting anything either from American tourists or local women, we stopped at the strip near the border in Tijuana. I don't know what I was thinking. I wasn't thinking. I got drunk and screwed a hooker off the street. We rented one of those little hotel rooms by the hour. She was great but I didn't use a condom, and this was when AIDS was really exploding. I was scared as hell. When I got home I called the Center for Disease Control in Atlanta and told them what I did and asked if they thought I had AIDS. They told me there was no way at that point to determine if I'd contracted HIV. They said I should be tested then, anyway, and again in six months. That's what I did. Thankfully, both tests were negative. But that scared me away from prostitutes and I haven't been with one since.

I want a regular woman. I'm divorced again and using the dating websites. I'm too old for the bar scene and don't like it anyway. Almost everyone on the dating sites seems to be looking for marriage made in heaven. Why can't women start posting the truth: I'm a twice-divorced, hardworking woman who can't hack marriage and am looking for a man to romance me until we get tired of each other.

Bondsman Bails Prostitutes

Paul recently sent an email regarding stories I've been writing about victims of sex trafficking. He had some opinions I disagreed with and wanted to discuss in a phone interview.

Paul – When I was a bail bondsman in the late seventies, I guarantee the young women I had contact with weren't coerced into prostitution, and lots of them enjoyed the sex. They also had a sense of belonging to a family made up of their pimps and the other girls.

Tom – I don't believe most women are going to enjoy sex with ten to twenty strange men a day, many of them much older than the women, plenty of them unattractive and unbathed, and quite a few violent. Victims of sex trafficking are slaves, flat out. There's a difference between sex trafficking and prostitution. Prostitution, for the most part, is voluntary.

P – I was definitely dealing with prostitutes, not slaves.

T – Tell me about some of the ladies you best remember.

P – Seven people stand out. The first was Roy, a mulatto pimp who worked as a janitor, more or less as a front. He had two girls. Both told me how much they loved him. One was a Latina from West Sacramento who was about twenty and one of the most beautiful women I've ever seen, still. She was relatively poor. The other was an attractive black woman, also about twenty, from south Sacramento. Her dad was affluent, had an important job in government.

T – How did he feel about his daughter's activities?

P – Once he came in to arrange bail. He said he was ashamed. I have daughters and can understand his feelings. She was arrested quite a bit, did a little jail time. It was a revolving door. The pimp usually paid the bail. It was very professional.

T – How much was bail?

P – At the time I think bail was about five hundred dollars, which meant a fifty-dollar bond. The Latina used to entertain a bounty hunter in my office all the time.

T – Right in the office?

P – In one of the other rooms, any room with a couch. I don't care whether it's politically correct, I think she liked the sex. Both girls wanted an adventurous life. They had a circuit. I don't know all the cities, but from Sacramento they went up and down Highway 99, like they do today, and they went to Las Vegas and Washington, D.C., and many points in between.

A few years later the black lady came in to visit me.

T – Why did she visit you?

P – To say hello. She said she'd moved on but had enjoyed her time in the business.

T – Who else?

P – I often had to bail out two white women who lived with their pimp in a nice trailer on the Sacramento River south of town. They were in their mid-twenties. They seemed to have an equal partnership. These weren't 4th and S types. These were hotel types, true professionals.

T – And they evidently kept getting arrested. How'd they turn out?

P – I don't know what happened to the women. The pimp was murdered in the late seventies in Rio Vista.

T – What happened?

P – He was either shot or stabbed.

T – Do you know why?

P – I'm not sure but think it was a redneck who was jealous of a black guy living with two beautiful white women.

T – That's six people. So there's one more memorable client.

P – I was actually kind of attracted to her. She didn't have a pimp and operated on her own. She lived in north Sacramento with her parents. They were very religious. One afternoon I took her to their house to get the money for bail.

"She's not getting anything from me," her father said. "I don't approve of what she's doing, and I'm not going to support it."

Being a prostitute was her choice. She had many other options.

T – What's your summary of these five ladies?

P – My impression was that all five got into it not willingly but wantingly."

On the Avenue

After watching The Trafficked Life, a disturbing documentary film, I called the director, Michael, and asked how he started learning about human trafficking? This is the essence of his reply.

I was out on Union Avenue in Bakersfield with a pastor who helps girls and young women get off the streets, and we started talking to a woman who told us she was a licensed medical technician. I recorded our conversation and have about forty minutes on tape. She was in her late twenties, a college graduate, had all the training and certification, and could have gotten a good job. Yet, she chose to sell herself. I tried to find out why but every time I asked questions too personal her eyes hardened. Otherwise, I could see in her eyes when she was happy. I concluded she wouldn't have been out there unless she'd been badly hurt somewhere else in life. Perhaps she was molested. I don't know.

She told me she made good money. And she didn't always have to have sex. She said sometimes men paid her just to rub her legs on them. People out there want a lot of different things.

I think she may have left the streets. Her niece had come to live with her, and she was getting tired of lying about why she was putting on a sweat suit and leaving every night and coming back the following morning.

Hooker Haven

A friend of the family, in the presence of his wife, offered the following job recollections.

I used to work the four to ten p.m. shift in a combination carwash and laundromat on south Union Avenue in Bakersfield. That's a rough area but also the most entertaining place I've worked. Every night, especially on weekends, hookers rolled in to use the bathrooms. I'm surprised the owner didn't have them locked so the ladies would have to get a key at the register. Lots of guys who came into the store weren't our customers. They just headed straight into the bathrooms. Afterward, I'd find condoms in there along with needles and syringes.

I finally told the owner, "Ladies of the night are using your restrooms for business."

We started locking the place up. A new employee, a guy in his teens, said, "I'm lucky I never walked in on them."

"It would've been educational."

My introduction came years earlier in Playa Del Rey where the wealthy live in beautiful apartments and moor their boats in the marina. I worked in the hospital emergency room. Late one night the doctor on duty told me, "I'm treating someone. Come in and conduct the interview."

A buxom woman in her twenties sat on the examination table. "What's the problem?" I asked.

"An asshole bit me."

"Where?"

She didn't answer.

"Go ahead and show him," said the doctor.

Lifting her skirt, she pointed between her legs.

My task complete, I left the emergency room and returned to my desk at the counter. On her way out the lady stopped and told me, "I'm usually with actors and rich guys who take me on their boats in the marina. Tonight I got the wrong dude."

The History Teacher

I was a teacher and loved helping high school students learn history. My favorite course, which I taught three times daily, surveyed the United States in the twentieth century. World War I could be interesting but got a bit slow in the trenches. Pace always accelerated with Prohibition and Al Capone and Babe Ruth and the Great Depression and Pearl Harbor and D-Day and Hiroshima and the Korean War and McCarthyism and the glorious but deadly sixties and the Vietnam War when the semester usually ended.

I'd studied history as a child in school, I'd read independently at home, I'd been a ceaseless learner in college and a dedicated teacher. I may have worked too hard and socialized too little, but that's not an alibi. History teaches us to accept consequences for decisions and avoid excuses. I still don't know how I could've perceived that dating Carl would be a disaster. Some say I must have been looking for trouble. I wasn't. I just wanted romance. Carl taught physical education at our school. He was handsome and fun and introduced me to the world of nightclubs and parties.

Every day, though I try not dwell, I wonder if the future would've been different if I hadn't gone to a party unlike the others. After Carl and I'd drunk quite a bit of wine, the host brought out some white powder and a tiny gold spoon and scooped some powder and snorted it in his right nostril then got another spoonful and snorted into his left. Saying, "Aahhh," he handed the spoon to Carl who tried it and encouraged me to go ahead and, frankly, I loved feeling like a hot ocean raced through my chest into my head.

After that we only went to parties where there would be white powder, and in a couple of months a guy named Adrian told us, "You'll never snort again once you smoke it."

I loved the intensity of an electrified brain and kept taking hits to maintain it and, when Carl wanted to leave, I said, "Go ahead. I'll get a ride from Adrian."

At school Carl ignored me but I didn't mind. For two weeks I'd been smoking every night with Adrian, who told me he couldn't keep paying so much. "Don't worry," I said. "I've got money."

I planned to cut back to weekends but found I was hurrying home to smoke all evening and much of the night and started getting to school late.

"Kathy, I need to speak to you after class," said the principal, Mr. Williams.

Tired and anxious to get home I entered his office, and he asked, "Is everything okay?"

"Everything's great."

"We can't permit any teacher to be tardy all the time. This is so unlike you."

"I understand and agree. I'll quit staying up so late planning lessons."

Instead I smoked more and started calling in sick. And I was sick, smoking two or three hundred dollars a day. In a year I spent my savings and mortgaged my house and a couple of months later got fired after my arrest for buying coke on the street in a notorious area. My parents, who'd figured things out, refused to make my house payments. I called Adrian and said, "Please help me."

"We'll help each other," he said. "I'm tired of delivering auto parts."

I sold my furniture and household items before foreclosure and moved into Adrian's apartment and tried what he said was necessary. The first customer was old and fat, the next young and thin, and plenty all ages were smelly and perverse.

"We can't keep doing this here," Adrian said.

"Where?"

"All over the West."

Name the cities. You'll be right. I entertained johns and Adrian sold coke and we stayed in old motels that, my academic instincts not entirely obliterated, I concluded were better than sleeping in the streets. I got arrested for soliciting a few times and simply left town. Adrian got arrested once on possession for sale and wasn't going anywhere. I returned to my hometown where my mother cried and so did my father as they told me I was a disgrace and slammed the front door. I checked into a homeless center and found plenty of ladies whose recent histories resembled my own. One of them, Diane, and I moved in with her brother and started working the streets. On a Saturday night a man pulled over, powered his window down, and said, "Oh, Kathy. I thought that was you and wanted to say hi."

"Nice to see you, Mr. Williams. Don't tell anyone at school, and I won't either."

After the Fight

I recently confessed, in an article about the fighter formerly known as Dwight Braxton, that in the summer or 1982 I was indigent and without cable TV and therefore desperate to find a place to watch his light heavyweight title fight against Matthew Saad Muhammad, the man he'd recently pummeled to take the title. After trying many restaurants and bars and even the recreation room of an apartment complex, I dashed into a flophouse, hoping I hadn't missed any blood-letting, and for five dollars rented a room for up to fifteen rounds. A perceptive reader, dissatisfied by my account of only a prizefight, demanded: "But what happened after the fight?"

At first, compelled by modesty, I replied with this post: "Wish I could tell you a wild party followed but I just went home to a studio-sized dump."

That's not what happened, and I'll tell you what did. Please don't think me a braggart. I know it was luck. It had never happened and hasn't since. But even in north Sacramento and other forlorn communities, a few people hit the jackpot.

I'd just turned off the TV and was preparing to leave the steamy room when a knock startled me and I pulled back curtains to behold two young ladies, a blonde and a red head, each clad in hot pants and delightfully inadequate blouses. I opened the door and said, "Hi."

"Your time's up," said Red. "Goodbye."

"Okay, sure. What's in the bag?"

"Rum and coke," said Blonde.

"Can I have a drink, please?"

"How much money you got?" she asked.

"Two dollars."

They laughed as if I were witty as young sensation Eddie Murphy.

"These drinks are for our dates," said Red.

"What time are you going you out?"

"We're not going anywhere," she said. "Our dates come to us."

"I don't use professionals, but I'm curious. How much do

you charge?"

"Twenty and up. Goodbye."

"Fine." I reached for the door but stopped as the phone rang. Blonde answered and listened awhile before saying, "Oh, shit. Jimmy's in jail. When's he getting out?"

She hung up. "What're we going to do?"

"You guys should go into a better kind of work," I said.

"So we can be rich like you," said Red.

Forget those who say it's easy to keep your confidence when you're broke. I didn't debate. I asked for a drink and said, "I'll pay both of you next payday."

"When's that?"

"Next Friday."

"Okay," said Blonde. "But don't run up too big a tab or Jimmy'll bust you when he's out."

My Fabulous Whorehouse

Houses are worth about half what you owe, gas is rocketing past four bucks a gallon, food's gotten so precious you're eating more lettuce than meat, and you've already told the kids to forget those elite universities and instead plan to attend local community colleges while they scramble for fast food jobs. Don't be ashamed. Hold your head high. Countermeasures are essential. You can justify your new plan. Countless Americans are researching the same venture. Go ahead and proclaim it: you'd love to open a whorehouse and already would have if you'd only known how. To survive, you just need special guidance. Don't worry. There's no charge. Just visit MyFabulousWhorehouse. com and read how happy and successful entrepreneurs sell hot tail.

Dear MFW,

Thank you for saying it. Thousands of us in this country have already done it and so have scores of thousands globally. I'm proud I improvised. My real estate agency in Newport Beach had lost half its annual sales, I'd defaulted on all of my inflated investment properties, and my principal residence, within sight of John Wayne's former place, was and is way under water. My wife, accustomed to leisure and luxury, had become quite tense and unresponsive, so I told her, "You want to live the way we had been, then help." She surprised and delighted me by agreeing to move with me into an apartment and use our beautiful home to host a carefully-screened group of wealthy men who were utterly spoiled by our staff of four beautiful Southern California ladies. At first we trusted the employees with receipts exceeding several thousand dollars a day, but that proved unwise. My wife volunteered to move back into our home, albeit into the maid's quarters, and is proving herself a shrewd and tough madam. In a few years we'll be out of debt, if we can maintain our primary business. And we're determined to do so. Whenever the police come – prompted by fussy neighbors, they've made a few visits in nine months – my wife simply explains the only way we can keep our home is by renting spare bedrooms to college students and young career women. We now instruct gentlemanly clients to avoid ostentatious entrances by calling shortly before arrival so our big garage door can be opened.

Johnny

Dear MFW,

It's always rankled me that I'm a better computer technician than Bill Gates, at least some who know have told me I am, but I'm neither the innovator nor entrepreneur he is, and have laid off as many people as I've hired since the late seventies. Some are now working in Asia. And my former wife, last I saw on Facebook, resides with one of them. I hope they're enjoying half the proceeds from the sale of our fine house, in which she, a math professor, had also dutifully invested. I now rent a modest three-bedroom home on a large wooded lot outside gloomy Seattle. Acknowledging that I'd probably always need some supplementary income, though not from a wife, I started another business and resolved to keep it small. I never have more than two women working for me and don't worry when there's only one. While I apply technology in the den, my most profitable ventures occur in two rear bedrooms and put about a grand a week in my pocket. I won't be living near Bill Gates but won't be in the street, either.

Fred

Dear MFW,

A bold and creative attorney I have been since my valedictory graduation from a distinguished law school several years ago. I have defended businessmen accused of beating their wives, professional women said to have clobbered their cheating husbands, and many of both genders who swore roadside sobriety tests were unscientific and inaccurate. Alas, many such businessmen are now bankrupt, the professional women earn less than they did five years ago, the drinkers are indigent, and all now use public defenders. As a result I've been cruising nightclubs and hotels and even a few scary streets of Sacramento, seeking advice from veterans. The ones with pimps I immediately eliminated. And no, I'm not therefore the pimp of ladies I've hired. I'm their attorney, working on a commission. In that capacity I last week rented three low-end motel rooms. Lots of bad dudes came around and few had money for my girls. I'd like to operate in private but the walls of my condominium are rather thin and my neighbors snooty. Maybe my office would be a divine location. There's parking in the back. What do you think?

Dick

Dear MFW,

I guarantee all of you I'm a bright girl and would have gone to college if I didn't have what I believe is a biological disorder, common to many, that always makes me drowsy and often puts me to sleep within ten minutes of starting to read. And I'm referring to textbooks, cookbooks, newspapers, literary fiction, romance novels. I don't like reading anything. As a result, I'm only able to get jobs as a waitress, department store clerk, or receptionist, and none of them makes me feel good or enhances my pocketbook. I figure I'll move up by getting married but always end up with bums and must listen to lectures by friends and relatives that women who go out with losers are seeking what they feel they deserve. I don't want to debate that. I want a drink and go to a popular disco in a large hotel and sail through the evening as I usually do, dancing and flirting, and spend the final hour talking to a sincere guy about ten years older than my twenty-five. He asks for my phone number and says, "I'd like to take you to dinner."

Maybe I should say yes. I consider it but instead reply, "I'm a pro."
"Excuse me."

"You pay, I play."

"I thought you were a regular woman."

"I'm a regular working girl."

"What do you do?"

"By day, I'm a secretary."

I feel his fantasies disappear and he rises before he sits back down and asks, "How much?"

"Depends what you want."

"For one time."

"Fifty," I say.

"Thirty."

"Fifty."

"Where?"

"I work exclusively in my apartment. It's safe and comfortable for both of us."

He follows me home and ends up spending a hundred. I decide to visit bars and discos around town three or four nights a week, rotating among many so I'm not too regular. Lately, I've been going places new to me where the guys are older and have the means to pursue a pretty young woman. I always sip a soft drink until someone starts buying. Even then, I stick to nonalcoholic beverages. I think I'm playing it smart. I require my clients to use condoms, and have already ordered two uncooperative guys to leave. I pray I'll never have to use the pistol hidden in my bedroom. Even after six months in this part-time venture, I only entertain two or three men a week so doubt my landlord and neighbors are suspicious. I'm starting to get some regular clients, once or twice a month guys, and earn as much as two thousand a month for not so much work and no worries about pimps. I just hope no guy who thought he was about to get lucky tells security.

Leticia

LEGAL

King of the Pimps

Times are hard after twenty years of truck driving and my truck breaking down along with my back and my bank account, and in my foreclosed home, which I'll soon have to leave – my wife's already taken the kids and left – I've had plenty of time for reading and by far the best and most exciting book I've read is *The Art of the Pimp* by Dennis Hof. I'd never heard of the guy until I saw him interviewed on several channels about what a great time Lamar Odom had been having at his Love Ranch whorehouse outside Las Vegas, and how surprised he was when two of his girls, who entertained Odom, found the former basketball star unconscious in bed. Hof, happy and relaxed despite the bad publicity, explained he doesn't allow cocaine or any other illegal drugs at his several establishments, but dishonest customers, maybe helped by conniving employees, can sometimes sneak things into even his clean places. Sitting next to a pretty but kind of rough-looking blonde, he introduced her as Caressa Kisses, which may not be her real name, and bragged he planned to have some action with her later on, and I guess it ain't bragging if it's true.

The Art of the Pimp ends before Lamar Odom's final visit – I guess he'd been there before – and I can tell you that Dennis Hof is the luckiest guy in the world and one of the most talented. As a young man he worked hard and owned several gas stations in Phoenix, and then sold those and moved to the Lake Tahoe and Reno area and bought some more, and got his real estate license and became a great salesman, and then a sales manager, not only in that area but near San Diego, and people all over the country hired him to sell their properties or time shares, and Dennis could drive his beautiful cars to any bar or nightclub and get beautiful women. And he did this even before he started buying whorehouses.

I live in Wisconsin, and my whole career I've just driven my truck from there to the East Coast, and partied with girls at plenty of truck stops but had no idea there were great places like Dennis Hof's. I'd like to buy my own but Dennis says it takes a million or so for the property and business and at least another million to fix it up and make everything first class. He's a pioneer like that. Before him, the cathouses were often trailers or rooms with old smelly carpets. Dennis says he's got the best whorehouse in the world, or sometimes it's just the United States. It's plenty good. He's got bars and swimming pools and pretty bedrooms and the girls have to keep them neat.

Oxford University asked Dennis to come and lecture about prostitution, and he did, telling the British they'd had illegal prostitution for a thousand years and still had the same problems, lots of disease and violence. In Nevada, where prostitution is legal except for big cities, there's never been a case of HIV in a registered brothel since state laws required the use of condoms during all sex acts. That doesn't sound fun but it's a good idea. Dennis often points out, during hundreds of TV and radio interviews – he's a big celebrity – that in Las Vegas hundreds of prostitutes are arrested on the streets every year, and ten percent are HIV positive. That doesn't make sense. Let Dennis Hof build some brothels in Vegas and clean the place up.

Dennis knows how to please the customers. He only hires classy girls. Yeah, some have been abused as kids but a lot fewer, he thinks, than among those working the streets. He's always looking for girls with special talent and gives them many private demonstrations how to please men. He's an expert who's screwed more than four thousand women, and even now, in his late sixties, diabetic, and about three hundred pounds, he says he gives young women – and he likes them very young and thin – eight orgasms before he even screws them. He loves sex and the more he gets the more he wants so he sometimes sets up a threesome, two girls and Dennis.

The girls at all his whorehouses of course look up to Dennis and call him Daddy and do everything they can to get him into bed. All his special girlfriends come from the business not only because they're young, thin, and beautiful but because Dennis believes they "understand the difference between love and sex." He loves his girlfriends, one at a time, but all of them eventually get crazy because he continues to get it on with the other girls. Those girlfriends are unreasonable since, from the start, Dennis has explained that's how it works, how it's always worked and always will. The women just love their big Daddy, who often gives them jewelry and phones and, most importantly, the opportunity to earn several hundred thousand dollars a year, or more, if they work hard, follow his principles of selling themselves and then loving the customer so well he'll come back and ask for her. The real stars have regular clients booking appointments with them online. It's all very first rate and modern.

Of course I want some of this, too, but can't pay thousands of dollars for sex. It kind of scares me when Dennis writes some guys have spent hundreds of thousands. But he says don't worry, ninety-eight percent of his customers are regular guys. When I get another truck, and a route that goes through Nevada, I'm going to visit one of his places. I think I'll be able to afford a quickie, but am not sure because when I called the lady told me they can't discuss prices over the phone. Besides, Dennis makes all his girls equal partners, a fifty-fifty split of service fees and tips, and the girls negotiate prices for all their parties. The only guy who doesn't pay is Dennis, who gets all he wants while earning more than a million bucks a year. That's what I call a stud.

Lamar Odom to the Hoop

It's late in a Los Angeles Clippers game early in Lamar Odom's rookie year but the young man, who just turned twenty, is given the mandate of an all star: take the ball to the basket every play. To facilitate this, coach Chris Ford tells the team's older players to clear the right side so Odom – six-ten, acrobatic, and a skilled ball handler – can drive and fake and twist to get inside for layups or draw fouls. Odom's in no way reluctant to assume this responsibility. He's in the zone, making plays and giving the Golden State Warriors, who appeared destined to win, more than they can manage. Ultimately, penetrating again, Lamar banks in another left-handed layup from the right side, the winning shot, and a small crowd at the Staples Center stands to cheer. They've witnessed something splendid and likely understand, as I do, that Lamar Odom will distinguish himself for a long time.

* * *

A year or two thereafter I wasn't alarmed when I heard Lamar had tested positive for marijuana. I'm not advocating anyone smoke pot or drink alcohol or take any other recreational drug. I'm advocating don't do it. But the hysteria about pot is baffling considering the devastation caused by alcohol and nicotine, society's two beloved legal, and lethal, drugs. Drinkers, informed people know, generally cause many more problems than pot smokers. What did strike me about Lamar Odom was how vulnerable he seemed as he asked his teammates and friends to forgive him. He was distressed and smoking more pot than anyone should. He may have been sedating himself to treat undiagnosed depression or a nervous disorder.

Then began a series of personal tragedies – relatives and close friends died, some prematurely, and his infant son succumbed to SIDS – that would wobble the strongest of souls, and Lamar Odom is perhaps a bit more delicate than most. Despite this he generally averaged about fifteen points, eight rebounds, and four assists a game, and played a key role coming off the bench for two Lakers championship teams. He'd joined the Clippers' big brother several seasons earlier, after a stop in Miami.

Many of us in fandom, despite lacking the perspective of people who knew Lamar well, should have suspected he had more problems than declining athletic skills when he played for the Dallas Mavericks, during the 2011-2012 season, and not only performed poorly but without conviction. He returned to the Clippers, where he'd started fourteen seasons earlier, and after one final mediocre year was out of the league. His personal difficulties became soap operatic when he married one of the Kardashians, Khloe, and opened his life on reality television, an inhospitable place for the sensitive. According to online gossip Odom and Khloe fought a lot and Lamar frequently visited other women and took cocaine, a drug about which there can be no compromise: one puff can stop a heart or rupture a vessel in the brain. On YouTube I recently watched a short video of Lamar from last summer. He appeared either intoxicated or hungover and, unlike the friend and teammate who was universally liked, even loved, he berated a reporter about how everyone had been mistreating him. Others can debate that point.

What's certain is that on an October 2015 weekend Lamar Odom began a binge that included cocaine and alcohol, and on Saturday phoned a shady place called the Love Ranch about an hour drive outside Las Vegas. He requested they come and pick him up. When a man's got a drug problem and lots of money, door to door service is an option. He arrived at the Love Ranch and hired two prostitutes who, for more than thirty-seven grand apiece, over the next three days gave him all the attention and cognac and herbal sexual enhancers and food one can imagine, and by Tuesday morning Lamar Odom was about dead, unresponsive in bed as strange fluids oozed from his nose and mouth. An ambulance was called and a woman stated Lamar had been using the substances above – but no coke after his arrival Saturday, of course, since the Love Ranch absolutely prohibits everything illegal.

Authorities may examine that issue but at this stage it's irrelevant to Lamar Odom, who's no longer unconscious or on life support and can sit up and talk a little to Khloe, who said she loves Lamar, and he indicated he loves her, too, and if that's true then he may have her help during what doctors say could be a lengthy recovery. Once he's out of physical danger, Lamar and his companions and doctors need to determine why a man who has so much in life retreated to a whorehouse where people watched him rot while raking in seventy-five grand for three days labor.

Notes: For a man constantly in the public eye as a professional basketball player and member of the Kardashian empire, Lamar Odom has not been much available to the public since his cocaine overdose at a Nevada brothel. He spent a few months recovering in a Los Angeles hospital where, according to unofficial reports (perhaps that means gossip), he couldn't walk for a long time and he spoke little and was hard to understand when he did communicate. I'm heartened that Lamar is getting the privacy he needs. Unfortunately, he also needed privacy when he and his gathering problems were being paraded on TV and the internet.

Birthday Bash

"Sweetheart, I'm giving both of us a special gift for my birthday," says Dan.

"What is it?"

"Let me show you."

From their spacious home in Carson City, where he lobbies in the state capitol and Ellen teaches psychology at a community college, Dan drives out of town and in ten minutes says, "All right, please slip this on," and hands her a black blindfold.

"You're kidding."

"No."

"I'm not putting this on."

"You'll spoil the surprise."

Looking seriously at her husband, she complies.

In a few minutes he pulls off the road and into a parking lot in front of a wrought iron fence and gate guarding some prefabricated one-story offices. Ellen reaches for her blindfold.

"Hold on."

"I want to see."

"Just a minute."

He hustles out and to the passenger side, takes Ellen's right hand in his left and helps her exit. Holding hands they walk to the gate where he pushes a buzzer.

"Welcome to the..."

"Don't say it."

"Who's this?"

"This is Danny Boy."

"Hello, Danny."

The gate buzzes unlocked, and he guides his wife to the front door a lady pushes open, and says, "Welcome to our home. Are you ready?"

"Yes."

She presses a button that rings bells down the halls, and in a couple minutes the reception area, furnished with two sofas and several soft chairs, fills with women. Some are wearing bikinis, others short pants and halter tops. Dan smiles at Candy, his favorite, and nods for her to escort them back to her bedroom.

"What's your birthday pleasure, Danny Boy?"

"Dan, what the hell is this?" Ellen says, pulling off her blindfold.

"Something I've always wanted."

"To bring me to a whorehouse?"

"For our love to be shared by another."

She spins and heads to the door but Dan takes her shoulders, gently, and says, "You often tell me how bored you are. Let's do something different."

"No."

"I'm going to make love to Candy."

"With a hooker, you call it making love?"

"The excitement I feel, yes."

Dan hands Candy his credit card and says, "Give it to the manager and leave my tab open."

"Back in two," she says.

"I'm leaving," says Ellen.

"So you can continue to be unsatisfied, like me, and make us both miserable by complaining."

Using his toes Dan peels off his slippers and unbuttons his shirt and takes it off and steps out of his pants and drops his underwear and says, "Get undressed."

"I'll get a damn divorce is what I'll do."

Candy returns, and Dan says, "I think we're going to have to tie Ellen in the chair."

"You'll go to jail, Dan. That's kidnapping," Ellen says.

"Maybe we better tie you up, Danny Boy."

"That's not what I want."

Candy steps into the hall and shouts, "Help." Four women rush into the room. As Ellen watches, the five force Dan into a chair, and Candy binds his hands with masking tape, and ties his feet the same way, and wraps a thin rope several times around each bicep and secures his torso with a few encirclements around it and the back of his chair.

"Thank you, ladies," Candy says, and they leave. She steps to

Ellen and kisses her open mouth, and they undress each other as they continue kissing.

"What the hell's this?" Dan says.

"Quiet, or we'll gag you," says his wife.

March Toward Legalization

Until this moment of online revelation none of my California constituents – I'm a state senator – knew I've been a regular customer up the road in the clean, regulated brothels of rural Nevada. My wife found out and left but our problems were with each other and had begun before my patronage of prostitutes. I'm not advocating that any man, or woman, purchase sexual services, but I'm unequivocally stating that if you do so don't do it on the streets where venereal disease and violence are rife. Go to legal places where the ladies are medically checked once a week and tested for HIV every month. Problem is, for safe and essential release, the only U.S. havens are in remote counties of Nevada. Few men in New York or Dubuque or Seattle are able to promptly avail themselves of this opportunity.

Now, I know a majority of Californians, including many holy johns, insist that prostitution must be kept illegal and on the streets, but in fact this blue-nosed policy creates an environment for contemporary slave owners, otherwise called pimps, to abuse and steal from young women and minors who because of sexual and emotional abuse during childhood are vulnerable to predators.

Don't presume we can solve the problem with endless vice operations and arrests. There aren't enough police and they're anyway needed to apprehend murderers, robbers, and rapists. And don't claim you can legislatively erase thousands of years of sexual desire and behavior. Ideally, men and women would marry as young adults and be passionate for decades. Most people know some who say they live that way. And a few doubtless do. But chemically-charged bodies often demand spontaneous relief we have neither the time nor opportunity to realize.

Don't believe only sad, lonely men pay for a good time. Countless fellows of note, married and single – actors, truck drivers, rock stars, legislators, mechanics, name a profession – risk far too much to dally on streets or in cars or frightening motels. Insist your political leaders acknowledge real needs and enable thousands of cities and towns to establish legal brothels. Demand that women undergo background checks before they become certified professionals and thereafter have regular medical exams. Take prostitution out of the gutter. Put it in a respected, or at least a regulated, place of business. Quit pretending having normal desires is avoidable. Be civilized enough to understand. And, for millions, acknowledge your personal history, if only to yourselves. My legislation will help.

WHERE WILL

WE SLEEP?

POVERTY

HOMELESS

Thanksgiving Dinner

Trees stand everywhere and seem greener here than in most places and the air is fresh and clean. It doesn't matter Los Angeles has the dirtiest air in the nation. Fifteen miles north, in Pasadena, you can breathe as trees caress you. This is indeed such an enchanting place that the railroad Huntingtons, and the Chandlers of the L.A. Times, and the Pattons of young George, Jr., and directors from Standard Oil, and many others built their primary residences here. With these privileged people came not merely a commitment to wealth and power but to culture and education. The Huntington Museum offers art treasures from both Old Europe and New America, and the Norton Simon Museum showcases a collection, anchored by Rubens and Van Gogh, superior to any acquired since World War II. Nearby is the former capital of live theater in the West, The Pasadena Playhouse, still a major venue. Also in the neighborhood is that powerhouse of scientific endeavor, Caltech. Go a little way on the other side of Old Town, the new district of stylish restaurants, shops, and galleries, and you come upon the Rose Bowl, Granddaddy of all big-game stadiums. And, of course, rolling through the heart of Pasadena is Colorado Boulevard, primary route of the robust Rose Bowl Parade.

A couple of blocks south of Colorado Boulevard, in an area of pretty brick and stucco offices and stores, rests shady Central Park where on this day more than two thousand people gathered to eat Thanksgiving dinner, though lunch would've been a more appropriate designation since the feast was scheduled for eleven-thirty. As I examined the food stacked on long tables forming a rectangle, I was reminded of an older Patton, the one in a uniform adorned by two pearl-handle revolvers. Prior to battle, he'd have appreciated such a precise and thorough buildup of supplies. Bearing handwritten labels on plastic or aluminum covers, all the sweet potatoes were huddled together, and so were the casseroles and beans and green beans and carrots and corn and mashed potatoes and pasta, and turning left the green salads and fruit salads and cranberry sauce and potatoes and hash browns, and turning left again the pies and cakes and cupcakes and cookies and brownies, and left again, soldier, the coffee and orange punch and fruit water and lemonade and water. Secure inside the perimeter, on a special set of tables, were the culinary stars of the event, the turkeys. A team of surgeons was carving them up.

About seventy yards away on a small stage stood a female disciple of Patton. She had been issuing orders into a microphone and listing objectives, not all being met, and she stated, "I'm a pregnant mother who's been working sixteen hours a day for two weeks, and I need people to help me clean up from three to four p.m. We already have plenty of servers. Now we need volunteers to wash dishes."

Within minutes, she announced the positions had been filled. I'd wanted to help but wasn't sure where I'd be during that period. I told a volunteer bright with red lipstick that I needed some stories.

"I have so much to be grateful for," she said. "I just saw a man here who lives in a park near our house. He can barely speak. I don't know what's wrong. I think he's got some sort of autism. These people need help and so often they don't know what they're eligible for. And many times they don't have any addresses where they can receive checks. The police are helping as much as possible. They regularly go around and talk to the homeless to make sure they understand all their options."

I'd been reluctant to approach the guests of honor, fearing they'd consider my questions intrusive.

"Hi," I finally said to a man in his forties. "Can I talk to you a little for a story I'm writing?"

"Sure," he said, shifting his cane to his left hand and offering me his right. One leg of his worn pants was puffed out by a swollen knee.

"Can you tell me why you came to Thanksgiving Dinner in the Park?"

"It's a nice, friendly atmosphere," he said. "I appreciate that. I was homeless a couple of years."

"You lived outside?"

"Yeah, my wife and I and our son. We'd been living in a motel for a few years. I did repairs there. Before that I was a union plumber a long time, worked at Disney, Warner Brothers, Hughes. The manager at the motel jumped in my face one day. I told him to bleep off. And he said get the hell out. We were on the street. Most of the time, we lived in a parking lot. All we had were blankets, an ice chest, and a grocery cart."

"How did you eat?"

"I panhandled. Stood on a busy street corner near downtown LA and held a sign."

"How much did you make doing that?"

"I usually brought in between forty and ninety bucks a day. The average was about fifty."

"What did your sign say?"

"This is exactly what it said:

'Homeless Family Turned Down By Welfare
Honest to God!
Can You Put Me to Work?
If not… Can You Please, Please Help?
We Are Sleeping on the Streets.'

"Dennis Rodman stopped and gave me money one day. So did Whoopi Goldberg and Nell Carter. Johnny Depp, too. And David Bowie. And Sinbad, the comedian, you know. And Eddie van Halen. And Tiny Tim, when he was alive. Nell Carter's dead, too. She gave me the most, twenty bucks."

"How about Rodman?"

"He gave me twelve, Whoopi ten."

"What about Johnny Depp and David Bowie?"

"Those guys only gave me about three dollars apiece. But hey, man, I appreciate it. Only about one out of every two or three hundred will help you."

"How did you shower and things like that?"

"We'd go to fast food restaurants, hospitals, any public places. Here, meet my wife."

She and I shook hands.

"We'd go to the store and buy Mexican dinners for two bucks apiece, and take 'em to a hospital and use the microwave there. We looked like we were regular visitors."

"Why didn't you get work, since you were a union plumber?"

"I couldn't because of injuries," he said. "My knee joint is bone on bone from an old martial arts injury. I used to go full contact. Both my knees are arthritic. I'd still be on the streets if my grandmother hadn't died about a year-and-a-half ago. She had sixteen grandkids, so I got a one-sixteenth share, about twenty-thousand dollars. It took six months to get the money, then I bought a van. That's what my wife and I are living in. We sent our kid, he's ten now, up to Washington to live with my mom. He had trouble every day in school here. Now he's advanced and they want to skip him a grade. We're gonna go up there and live in a couple of months. I've still got enough to pay for about a year's rent. That'll give me time to get back into plumbing, maybe do some landscaping, and some real estate."

"You look pretty good," I said. And he did, except for a few missing teeth. I didn't need to ask where health care is for those on the streets. And I didn't want to mention I smelled alcohol on his breath.

"Thanks. I just gave myself a haircut last week. For seventeen years my hair'd been almost down to my ass."

"I appreciate your time," I said, shaking his hand.

I knew who I'd talk to next – the man in his sixties who'd been listening to us. His gray hair was neatly combed straight back and he looked like a former businessman distressed by significant but intangible difficulties.

"Sir, can you tell me why you came to Thanksgiving Day in the Park?"

"Poverty."

"Are you retired?

"Not if I can get a job."

"What kind of work did you do?"

"Sales and insurance."

"What happened?"

"Did you watch *Frontline* last week?" he asked.

"No."

"Did you read *Fortune* magazine last month?"

"No, I didn't see that one."

"It's all about Wal-Mart. They're turning the United States into a Third World country."

"How are they doing that?"

"They only pay their employees – and I'm talking about full-time employees – about seven dollars an hour with no health care. Then when the employees get sick, they dump them on the welfare system. I know lots of Wal-Mart employees – full-time employees – who are on food stamps and live in section eight housing. It's not only Wal-Mart. All our jobs are either digitized or sent overseas. It's greed and plantation economics. They're closing down the American Dream."

I shook his hand and said, "Good luck."

Staring up the long line, proud but wounded, he said, "Sure."

Next I approached a well-groomed lady in her fifties. In Spanish I said, "Good morning. May I please talk to you for a little while?"

"Yes," she said, smiling.

"Where are you from?"

"Guatemala City."

"How long have you been in the United States?"

"Eight months."

"Why did you come today?"

"A friend invited me to The Day of the Turkey. I've never seen anything like this."

"How do you like the United States?"

"It's enchanting, beautiful. In Guatemala we have many natural resources, rivers, lakes, hills, and oil. But life is hard because the government doesn't try to help people. The politicians rob millions and millions from the people. I'm very happy to be here."

To complete the rainbow of interviewees, I approached a young man.

"Hi, can you please tell me why you're here today?"

"Yes, to get some food. It's a good charity."

"Where are you from?"

"South Africa."

"Are you a student here?"

"Yes, I'm studying film production at LA City College. After that, I'd like to go to USC or UCLA."

"Those are great film schools. Do you want to direct feature films?"

"No, I want to specialize in editing documentaries about the environment. I'm also interested in writing and photography. I'm particularly concerned about the destruction of forests."

"Yeah, the Bush administration is pretty bad about that."

"I'm not talking about the United States. The United States is way ahead. Your forests are well-maintained. You have controlled cutting. The environmental problems here are related to the emissions of gases. That's different. In Africa they're cutting down forests because they use wood to cook. They need to find alternatives. It's necessary everywhere to find a balance between human beings and animals."

"You look like you're in good shape," I said.

He didn't respond.

"I mean, lots of people here have problems, drinking and so forth."

"I'm fine," he said.

"Thanks a lot."

Turning, he moved into long lines where two thousand people moved toward Thanksgiving dinner.

Christmas Eve

"This way, gentlemen, in the far corner," said a male employee, taking a ticket from each.

Most of the men had beards or several days' growth and were bundled in a big coat, or a jacket and a coat, or a sweater and jacket and big coat. Almost all wore caps or hoods or both, and lots walked slowly on crutches or leaned on canes. Quite a few others moved unaided but in the painful, uneven way of the infirmed.

"That's right, gentlemen," said a volunteer. "Just have a seat right here."

They entered a large Christmas-decorated room where volunteers shoveled pizza, spaghetti, and salad onto paper plates whisked to their tables.

I walked to the ticket taker and asked, "Did you pass those out earlier in the day?"

"Yeah," he said. "That way everyone gets to eat once. Otherwise, some would come through twice and some wouldn't get to eat."

Almost four hundred were expected this Christmas Eve, and the pizzas were stacked high in boxes, donated every year by Little Caesar's. No one had to worry I'd snatch a plate, not at this party. I was looking for someone to write about. I watched a man point his TV camera at a table of diners. A female volunteer told me a newspaper reporter had been there awhile ago and departed after interviewing the director of the event. Evidently, the scribe hadn't known the best stories churned inside those cleaning their plates.

A few women now entered. They comprised less than ten percent of the party. I studied the groups of rather somber diners, waiting for people to finish before I approached. Who looked like an intriguing character? Rather, who sounded like one? A difficult choice became easy when I heard a woman rail about treatment she'd received this night and in the past. She sat at a table with another woman and a teenage boy. "Excuse me, ma'am, may I please speak to you?"

She looked at me but didn't answer.

"I'd like to talk to you for a story I'm writing."

"You gonna use my name?"

"Not if you don't want me to."

"Call me Evelyn, but that's not my name."

"Thanks." I pulled back a chair and joined them at the round table with a white paper tablecloth. "Have you been homeless long?"

"I've been back and forth the last nineteen years. I've got no resources, no money. I've been income-less the last nine years. I've been punched, mugged, hit in the head with bottles, raped. I never know where I'm gonna sleep at night. I don't know where I'm gonna sleep tonight. I walk around cold and tired and try to find a safe place, even if it's not. I sleep in abandoned houses, buildings, alleys, parks. They're not safe. I don't have nowhere to go. There's so much violence in the streets."

The boy and his mother finished dinner and departed.

"Evelyn, don't you have family to stay with?"

"No. Two of my sisters are taking care of five of my six kids. I signed them over. The other's twenty-one now, and I just became a grandmother."

"Can't the children's father help you?"

"No, my second husband's the father of the first five kids, and he's helping them with child support. I don't want anything from him. He was the worst of my three husbands. I married one right after the other and never bothered divorcing. I was a bigamist. I'm still married to the first and third husbands, but I divorced the second. He was a violent alcoholic and a black belt in karate."

"Jesus, did he hurt you?"

"Yeah, but I learned karate, too."

"Still, he's a man."

"I got quicker and he got slower. He had crippling arthritis in addition to being an alcoholic. And he started getting fat."

"Are you going to see your kids tomorrow for Christmas?"

"No."

"They live far away?"

"They live right here in Bakersfield."

"Then why not?"

"Look how I look. I'm ashamed of my appearance. I have no self-esteem. These are the only clothes I have, what I'm wearing. I can't carry anything. But I have everything I need for hygiene in my purse – toothbrush, toothpaste, comb, and deodorant."

A number of Evelyn's teeth were missing and most of the others had rotted down to darkened nubs. With a shaking hand, she picked up her tea and almost spilled it.

"Why don't you stay here at the The Mission?"

Crying now, she said, "They used to be coed but they've put women out on the street."

"They have a residential program for women," I said. "I talked to them about it. It sounds pretty good."

"I don't want to be in a program. They tell you you can't this, can't that, can't eat or sleep but when they tell you. I don't want that."

"Why don't you stay at the Bakersfield Homeless Center?"

"They eighty-sixed me."

"What happened?"

"About nine years ago I had my five kids and was pregnant. I was pushing my shopping cart that had everything I owned in it, and the security guard said, 'You can't bring that on the premises.' I went upside his head, and they called the police. I've tried to get back in but my name's in their computer and they won't let me in."

"What about work? Can you get a job to get off the streets?"

"I have a poor work history. I can't deal with people. I hate crowds and stress. And I don't have any ID. I've worked in some big retail stores but never made it more than a couple of months."

"What about high school?"

"I went to South High. I was a Rebel. I ran on the track team and was one of the fastest girls in the state in the hundred yard dash."

"Did you graduate?"

"They kicked me out. I was working in the student store and a white girl called me a nigger and spit on me. I beat her till she bled in the face. Then I had to go to two continuation schools. I got my GED at Bakersfield Adult School in 1984."

"How old were you?"

"Twenty-two."

"Okay, there you were at age twenty-two, young, with a high school diploma. What happened?"

"I've been abused all my life," she said, crying again. "I've always had a lot of anxieties and stress. I can't sleep. I've got bad nerves. I can't sit still. I'm fidgety."

"So what happened?"

"I started soliciting, loitering, using drugs."

"Which drugs?"

"Alcohol, pot, cocaine. I went to prison twice for selling rock cocaine. I was in prison a total of four years. I was also in jail here. They gave me elavil and other medications that helped me sleep. But when I got out I couldn't pay for pills. I haven't been back to jail in six years, and I've had the worst problems of my life. But I'm clean now."

"How long have you been clean?"

"Two weeks."

"Listen, you've got to get some medical help."

"I've been in two recovery homes. When I left I used drugs as much as I could when they came at me. Street people offer anything bad before something good. They're wolves in sheep's clothing. They prey on people."

"You've got to get medical treatment, and you've got to have a plan."

"I'm gonna try to get SSI disability again. They turned me down the first time because I was on drugs. They won't take you anymore if you're on drugs. I'm gonna keep bothering SSI. I need the help. I'm scared of being on the streets. I'm scared of somebody doing something to me. I want to live and let live. Sometimes I victimize people, too. My wrist is still sore from two weeks ago when I beat a lady.

"Last New Year's Eve I was sitting in another lady's house. She wasn't home but she'd told me I could stay there. And her friend – they must've been lesbians – told me to leave. I said I just wanted to wait and ask her if I could stay. And this lady beat me in the head with an ashtray. Blood was everywhere. They took me away in an ambulance. It's one year coming up and it's haunting me again. It's hard to let go. Then I lash out."

Tears again rolled down Evelyn's once-attractive face.

"I heard they're having a party for you guys tonight," I said.

"Yeah, it's next door," she said, standing. "Remember, don't use my name or I'll kill you."

"I promise."

"God bless you," she said, and walked through an almost empty room toward the exit.

New Year's Eve

On New Year's Eve I drove down Baker Street, long the hub of commerce and family activity in east Bakersfield until money and development in town moved west, and the area began a long decline that ruined numerous businesses and exploded several years ago when arsons consumed some of the surviving enterprises and a couple of flophouses where a few residents died of smoke inhalation. Now the nearby park where people loitered day and night, drinking and taking drugs, has been bulldozed, and efforts to revitalize the area are underway. This will continue to be a difficult task, as building fast continues to the west, and plans are progressing to develop thousands of new homes further east, where there are hills in this otherwise flat and parched community in the Central Valley of California.

Just off Baker Street, a couple of blocks down 21st, stand several buildings that comprise The Mission, provider of food and shelter for the homeless, the addicted, the paroled, and downtrodden. Those with the most critical needs can, without explaining their personal history, be admitted to the homeless intervention services facility. For more advanced treatment, there is the discipleship residential program, administrated and housed in separate buildings on campus. I parked at the appointed address and walked in to be greeted by a man and a woman. He was freshly-shaved, his mustache neatly trimmed, and looked businesslike in a tie and jacket. She glistened in fresh makeup and a stylish blouse and coat.

"I'm a little early," I said. "Can you tell the disciples I'm here for the interview?"

"That's us. I'm William, and this is Alice."

"Oh – you're certainly in fine shape."

"We weren't when we arrived," he said.

They escorted me into a small room next to the chapel and dining facility, where other disciples were starting to gather. I sat facing William and Alice.

"What drugs did you use?" I asked.

"Heroin," William replied.

"Methamphetamine," said Alice.

"I began shooting heroin in the seventies for about four years before going back in the eighties for three years. I'd cleaned up using various programs, including methadone. During the nineties I used at least seven years. The people at my county office never detected I was using but I was late all the time and often had to rush out early to make connections. My life at home hadn't been healthy, either. My ex-wife was a pharmacist, and she stole pharmaceuticals and used and sold them."

"Is she still doing that?" I asked.

"No, she's cleaned up and is very religious."

"Do you have any children?"

"I have a seventeen-year old daughter."

"You see her often?"

"I'm really not allowed to have any contact."

"What happened at work?"

"I lost my job and was homeless about four years."

"What was it like living on the streets?"

"Everything is day to day. The first thing you have to do is take care of your physical need. Drug addiction supersedes everything, and you never know what's in store. I was involved in at least a dozen armed robberies, and I burglarized houses, stole from stores, forged checks, panhandled, whatever. I was using as much as two hundred dollars of heroin a day and figured it would be easier to get that by selling. I'd buy a quarter-piece – that's a quarter ounce, six or seven grams – for one ninety-five to three-fifty, and break it into dime bags, eight to eleven per gram, and sell several hundred dollars worth and keep the rest for personal use.

"When you're 'Holding the Bag for Sale', people will cater to you – until you run out. In exchange for lodging, you give them heroin at night and in the morning so they don't have to go out and do the things you do. But people get lazy and start stealing your drugs, or their friends do. This arrangement never lasts longer than two to seven days.

"So I was often back on the streets and committing crimes, which I couldn't stomach. I never got caught for armed robbery or burglary, but did some time in county jail for petty theft, bad checks, and boosting stores."

"What's boosting?" I asked.

"It's taking items from stores for resale."

"What's the longest you were in jail?"

"I was in jail six months, but went to prison sixteen months for sales and possession."

"You've been clean since your last incarceration?"

"No. The day I was released – December fifteenth – I didn't contact my parole officer. I went on the run and straight to a connection, and I was back doing armed robberies and burglaries. I knew I had to quit or I'd get struck out and twenty-five to life, or worse."

"What did you do?"

"I came to The Mission. I'd been here before but hadn't been able to stay clean long. This time, though, they saw I was committed to changing my life, and not just because the alternative was a parole violation and going back to prison. But you can't enter the Discipleship Program when you're on drugs. I'd used thirty minutes before I returned. So at first I had to stay in the homeless intervention services facility here."

"Withdrawal from heroin is pretty tough, isn't it?"

"Yes. I couldn't sleep and was nervous and had diarrhea all the time."

"You made it cold turkey?"

"Not completely. I had to go out a couple of times for a little heroin to get a little taste to stabilize me while my body adjusted. In a couple of weeks I tested clean and was ready for the program."

While heroin is the diabolical downer, methamphetamine is the unrelenting upper, and Alice thus struggled on the opposite side of intoxication.

"I was on drugs for thirteen years and sold them the last eight. I was always doing runs, picking up chemicals and supplies, transporting meth to Arizona and Las Vegas, all over."

"And you made enough to stay off the streets?"

"Yes, I could always pay the rent, and buy food and clothes for my three kids. And I maintained hygiene. But I was using all the time and never came down. I learned how to eat and sleep on it. At the time, that felt normal. A lot of people thought I wasn't on drugs. But my oldest son knew why I was leaving and returning all the time. He had to take care of my two youngest kids.

"I began to pray I'd get in trouble to force me into recovery. I'd lost thirty pounds and was really scrawny. When I was busted last year I was thirty-five years old, but I thought I was thirty-seven. That's what I told the police. I was sentenced to a year in jail and a year in this program. I was only in jail four months until I got early release because of the Fed Cap Kick."

"What's that?"

"That's when there's overcrowding and they release the least dangerous inmates."

"Then you came here."

"I went back on drugs a couple of times first. Then I came here and that's been a blessing. They're teaching me how to walk with God. They keep me in the bible. Last year I couldn't spend Christmas with my children."

She stopped talking a moment and tried to suppress tears.

"This year I got to spend seventy-two hours with them."

In addition to daily prayer, bible studies, and Alcoholics Anonymous and Narcotics Anonymous meetings, the recovery program is founded on work therapy. The disciples, who usually haven't been able to maintain regular jobs, are required to put in daily shifts as cooks and dishwashers, workers in the maintenance and housekeeping departments, salespeople and stockers in the thrift store, mechanics, or as receptionists. William has ten months in the program and will graduate in two months. As a senior disciple, he is allowed to sleep in a room with only three others. Most of the other sixty-six disciples currently in the men's program sleep ten or more in each of several rooms dispersed in a building that long ago was a hotel. William has also earned more responsibility and works for the administration, overseeing the program office, instructing new disciples, and taking people to doctors and other appointments. Alice works in an office, using various computer programs. The women's housing facility looks like a small college dormitory; two to four disciples share each room.

"When I graduate in March, I'd like to work with elderly people in a convalescent home," she said.

"What about you, William?"

"At first, I'm planning to stay here as a grad student. I want to make sure to avoid triggers."

"Triggers?"

"Things that set you off, old memories, old failures, the wrong people, places, and things. That's why when I'm finished here I'd like to move away to a new place, maybe somewhere in the mountains, like Reno."

"I'm going to stay in Bakersfield," Alice said. "I'll be bringing my two youngest kids from Ridgecrest to live with me. The oldest is doing well in high school there, so he can stay as long as he continues to get good grades."

"What's going on at the party tonight?" I asked.

"They used to have dancing but that led to fraternization between the men and women, and we're not allowed to fraternize, on or off this campus, during our year in the program," said William. "Tonight, everyone will be in our chapel and expected to give testimony and pray."

"I don't know what it's like to party sober," Alice said. "I'm going to find out tonight."

Cycle of Abuse

Edward's cell phone rang and he slid a strong hand into overalls to retrieve it and talked a couple of minutes before finishing: "Okay. Thanks. I'll see you this afternoon.

"That was my wife. Our divorce is going to be final soon but she's driving to Bakersfield to take me back to Tulare for the weekend. We've been talking by phone, trying to work things out. We've got a lot of stuff to deal with."

* * *

Edward's parents divorced when he was two-years old and his mother gained custody and in a few years married a man who drank all the time and loved to take off his belt and whip the boy at least once a day. He also regularly pummeled his wife, and at a party one night broke her jaw and ripped her shirt off. The mother, fearful and diffident, took no action. Neither did authorities. In a corrupt and drug-ridden area in rural Oregon they were often unresponsive to domestic violence. Nine-year-old Edward begged his mother to call his father, who agreed to take the boy in with his new family of a wife and her three children.

"She made me clean horse stalls, feed animals, wash dishes, everything," Edward said. "And her kids didn't have to do anything."

"Didn't your father try to help?" I asked.

"He worked all day as an electrician and came home tired, ate, and went to bed."

"Was he nice to you?"

"When he was with me, but that didn't happen much."

Tense and unhappy, Edward sought satisfaction in contact sports and weightlifting. As a fifteen-year old sophomore he bench pressed three hundred twenty-five pounds. On the football team he played linebacker and fullback, where tough kids roam. He also won the Oregon small school wrestling championship, and carried aggression off the mat.

"I got into lots of fights," he said. "Someone would give me the wrong look, put me down for the clothes I wore, lots of stuff. One guy had been antagonizing me for a long time, and one day playing basketball in the gym he yelled, 'That was a fucked up shot.' He thought he was popular and could get away with it. I flattened him with one punch to the mouth. Did five thousand dollars damage to his braces. The police didn't arrest me since I was a minor and a first-time offender. They cited me, and I had to do two months of community service in a dog kennel. The school also expelled me the final month of my sophomore year.

"I didn't get in any fights my next year, but I had arguments with my teachers and let them know I didn't want to do some things they expected. I spent a lot of Saturdays in detention. My grandfather told me I better cool it or I'd never get anywhere in life; I'd either be dead or in prison."

Edward won his second state wrestling title as a junior, ran and tackled hard as a senior, his fourth straight year as a gridiron starter, and culminated his high school athletic career by winning a third wrestling championship. In the classroom, he maintained a three-point-five grade point average.

"In math class that spring, this guy was running his mouth, putting me down," Edward said. "Afterward, outside, I went after him. He ran, and I tripped him, and he fell and acted like he was really hurt. This time they kicked me out of school permanently. I never graduated. And I was arrested and spent ten days in jail. I hated it. I also had to do fifteen days of community service."

"Were alcohol and other drugs involved in your problems?"

"No, I hadn't done much of them at all."

"What happened then?"

"I went to alternative school a couple of hours a day and started running with the wrong crowd. The small town I lived in was boring. I had no job, nothing to do. I started drinking a lot, smoking weed, dropping acid, and, worst of all, using crank. It was fun at first, but it ate me up. Over the next two years I used it almost every day and my weight went from two hundred pounds to one-forty. I was living with my grandparents by then, and stealing their checks and forging them. They told me they didn't trust me anymore."

"I guess not."

"Yeah, I knew I had to get away and start over. I'd heard about the discipleship program here at The Mission. I stepped off the bus January fourteenth a few years ago, and came straight here. We studied the bible, went to AA and NA meetings, but I was kicked out after three months."

"Why?"

"You're not allowed to stay out overnight, but my girlfriend, Sue, needed help moving, so I went with her."

"Sounds like you got a girlfriend right after coming to Bakersfield."

"Yeah, I met her through her parents. They were in the same program."

"So you were without a place to stay? Is that when you entered the homeless intervention services?"

"No, not then. I moved in with my girlfriend and worked for the landlord. I stripped and waxed floors."

"Were you using crank?"

"No, my girlfriend made sure I stayed sober. And when I turned twenty-one, three years ago, I started working as a bouncer at Trout's nightclub in Oildale" – a Bakersfield suburb like a place from the Great Depression.

"I hear Trout's is rough."

"It was pretty violent. On New Year's Eve I was trying to escort a big drunk cowboy out of the club, and he turned and punched me in the ear. I punched back, lots of others jumped in; it was the domino effect. There were five bouncers, and we fought nonstop for forty-five minutes. Someone called the police, and they came but wouldn't come in. They waited outside as we physically removed one guy at a time."

Three weeks before this incident, Sue and Edward had become parents of a baby girl. She began pressuring him to leave the unhealthy workplace, particularly after he stayed out all night with a female customer.

"Sue didn't believe me, but I swear I couldn't do anything with that woman," he said. "My emotions wouldn't let me. We just slept on separate sides of the bed."

"That's hard to imagine."

"Really. I wanted to prove I loved Sue, so I quit Trout's and married her a couple of months later. We moved in with her aunt and uncle. I worked for a landscaping company."

"How long did that last?"

"Two years. It paid the bills. We got our own apartment, but my wife and I really started arguing. I suspected she was being unfaithful since she was always on the phone late at night; she never showed me any affection."

"You weren't intimate?"

"That's right. She said I was always gone working, and part of it was pay back for that night I left her. I found out she'd been with at least three guys. One night this guy called and said, 'Is Sue there?'

"'No, she's supposed to be at work.'

"'Who's this?' he said.

"'I'm her husband.'

"'What are you doing there?'

"'I live here.'

"My wife and I had a lot of problems about that and other stuff. She was always nagging me, saying I didn't spend enough time with my daughter and her. I'd get sick of it and start punching holes in walls, throwing chairs through windows. And I told her: 'Be thankful that was a wall and not you.' She'd still keep following me around and nagging. Finally, she moved in with the guy who'd called. He was old as hell."

"How old?" I asked.

"At least thirty-seven."

"That's not old."

"Old enough to be her father. I had to get away, and headed back to Oregon."

"How'd things go there?"

"Terrible. I stayed with my mom; her new boyfriend treated her like crap, just like every man she's known. He called her fat, ugly, told her no one wants her."

"Unfortunately," I said, "quite a few people fall into patterns like that."

"I took the bus back to Bakersfield last September and came right here to homeless intervention services, and started doing crank every day.

"Right here?" I asked.

"Usually in a park near here. Anywhere, really."

"Did you snort the crank?"

"I smoked it, mostly. Here, look at my hand."

He displayed scar tissue from a third-degree burn inflicted as he obsessively applied fire to an empty pipe.

"Did your wife know about all this?"

"Not really. She was living with the old guy and wouldn't let me see my daughter. I had to go to court. And she still refused to let me, so I went back and the judge said, 'Let him see her or you're going to jail.'

"She claimed I'd abused her when we lived together, but I just laughed and the judge knew I hadn't. She admitted I'd never harmed our daughter. The judge also knew I wasn't the one who'd given her the black eye she had in court. Her unemployed boyfriend did that."

A few months ago Edward was ready to return to the program of spiritual healing offered by the discipleship. One month later he was out.

"What happened this time?"

"I wanted to go to my stepsister's wedding in South Carolina. I stayed three months, doing construction. I just got back to Bakersfield in May, and came right here to the homeless intervention center."

"What plan do you have to get out of here?"

"Right now, I'm working in a dog kennel, doing maintenance and grounds keeping. And I'm applying for jobs with construction companies. There's a framing company in Bakersfield where I think I can get on. They pay minimum wage to start, with a raise after three months."

"So you'd be able to get out of here then?"

"Maybe soon. If my wife and I can work things out, I'd live with her in Tulare. She's got family there and a job in a fast food place. I could commute an hour each way to work."

"What if you can't work things out with her?"

"Living in a homeless shelter isn't as bad as people think. You get three meals a day, a shower, clothes, a place to sleep. I'll be fine."

Homeless on the River

For days I had looked forward to yet dreaded leaving a soft bed at four on a winter morning to shower, slap on sunscreen, eat a good breakfast, and drive across town to the east side, where poverty is prevalent and The Mission draws most of its clients. I'd volunteered to complete one of dozens of three-person teams assigned to visit where many homeless in Bakersfield live, pass out water and hygienic supplies, interview those willing, and fill out census forms containing relevant information about their lives. Most of the teams didn't have to arrive until six. They'd be canvassing the city. We who volunteered for the Kern River zones had to start at five.

In a large meeting room I met the leader of our team, a counselor for Kern County, and the other member, a college student pursuing his master's degree. Another man, a photographer, joined us for graphic documentation of those who exist under conditions most never witness. We loaded supplies into the trunk of a county vehicle and departed. I can assure organizers at The Mission, and the homeless collaborative overseeing these efforts, that in January it's unnecessary to start searching so early. It was dark and cold and sunrise almost two hours distant when we parked at Beach Park, and no homeless people were about when we walked the levee overlooking the dry bed of the Kern River we couldn't see. We moved down to the bike path and dirt trails stretching beside the riverbed but still saw nothing and returned to Beach Park and admired body-contoured riding suits and stylish helmets of bicyclists who arrived in cars, removed their cycles, and in groups headed on what the photographer, generally a participant, said is a vigorous twenty-mile ride in about an hour.

The counselor drove onto the levee road from whence we'd walked and then down to the bike trail, and despite our assignment to scour the south side of the Kern River he decided, based on a decade of experience, to look on the north side where he surmised there'd be more action. He parked on an elevated road short of the other side, as the eastern sky showed a little pink, and during one stretch we walked not on trails or paths but in the riverbed, moving over a series of stones slick and jagged. The other men negotiated them as if on flat ground but I almost fell several times and said, "I'm coming back a different way."

Soon after reaching the north bank of the Kern, and a clear morning brightened, we began seeing numerous shopping carts, including fashionable red models bearing FoodMaxx labels, and also noted a pile of crushed spray paint cans sniffed dry, sections of trees and bushes charred by campfires uncontrolled, and, my favorite, a single pink high heel shoe. I was enthused when we spotted our first campsite. An empty sleeping bag lay under a tree and two red shopping carts stood next to a silver one loaded with firewood. Down the road a bit, heading west toward Highway 99, we found a place with no one home and a message there'd be no return: clothes, sheets, cans and other food containers, plastic and canvas tarps, and the detritus of an exposed life littered an area otherwise dominated by a tree and surrounding bushes. In a little while, we found another camp where trees braced a canvas shelter and a tent housed a bicycle. Shoes in good condition rested nearby.

"Hello, Kern County," said the counselor. "We're here to take the census for the homeless alliance. We have cigarettes, water, and some health products. Can we talk to you?"

I also tried to coax a response. No one replied but I felt a human presence. On we walked. In a few minutes a man approached us on a bicycle.

"You guys scared my wife," he said.

"We're just trying to get information so the county can provide more benefits for the homeless," said the counselor. "Do you have time to answer a few questions for our census survey?"

"I got nothing but time."

Carrying the surveys on a county clipboard, propped on my note-taking folder, I stepped to the man and said, "I'm Tom. Are you ready to begin the survey?"

"Sure."

There were twenty-seven numbered questions, some with several parts, requiring about thirty-five inquiries and answers. I condensed the highlights below:

"Where did you sleep last night?"

"Right back there," he said.

"How long have you been homeless this particular time?"

"We've lived two years in the same spot. Sometimes the cops used to come over and tear up our camp, but they don't mess with us anymore."

"How old are you?"

"Thirty-seven."

"Are you Hispanic or Latino?"

"I'm white."

"Before you were eighteen, were you ever involved in the justice system?"

"Yes."

"Have you ever participated in Alcoholics Anonymous or Narcotics Anonymous or a drug treatment program?"

"Yes."

"Have you been arrested more than once for a DUI, public intoxication, drug possession or other drug offense?"

"Yeah."

I read him a daunting list of drugs: alcohol, marijuana, cocaine/crack, meth, heroin, and prescription drugs.

"Meth," he said.

"Have you ever been hospitalized for a mental or emotional disorder?"

"No."

"Are you currently being treated for a mental or emotional disorder?"

"Yes."

Then I read some potential problems: valley fever, tuberculosis, Hepatitis C, HIV, diabetes, asthma, and heart disease.

"Hepatitis C."

"Do you receive Social Security Insurance, disability insurance, or other pension or state disability payments?"

"SSI."

"Do you have any children living with you here?"

"No."

"Can I print your name here and have you sign below and give us some contact information, a phone or an email, so the county can contact you if you're eligible for more services."

"Yes," he said. I handed him the survey and he provided the information.

"Thanks."

"Want a cigarette?" said the counselor.

"Sure."

This man still appears in reasonable health, I thought, but older than thirty-seven. Shortly, another man arrived, pushing a cart on the trail. He said he'd been homeless ten years, with no sheltered breaks. He'd also been, and perhaps remains, a meth addict, and half his teeth were missing and the survivors appeared to be in decay. He'd suffered from valley fever, tuberculosis, and asthma, and about his heart he said, "I don't know." He thanked us for the water, cigarette, and supplies – toothpaste and toothbrush, soap, shampoo, and socks – and slowly walked toward an unpromising future.

A freight train, pulled by several engines and laden with heavy supplies, roared by and marked our westernmost advance. Heading back we avoided the slippery rocks and arrived at a weir that could decorate a Beverly Hills patio: the main concrete wall bore bricks painted by a talented artist who made illusory bricks prettier than real ones. The artist also had the facility to paint realistic blue and white tiles on a side wall aglow this morning.

Back in the county car I checked my cell phone and concluded, "Only eight-thirty and I'm tired. It's got to be hell living out here day and night for months or years at a time."

The counselor drove back to the south side of the Kern River and began to identify campsites far from dirt roads and bike paths. "You guys up for going over there?" he several times asked. We always agreed to walk through a couple hundred yards of sand and powdery dirt leading to trees or bushes anchoring tents or walls of canvas. Dead tree limbs and bushes usually strengthened the perimeters. The photographer sometimes walked with us, others he wandered and snapped pictures.

I hope he got an image of a large camp featuring several long tarps hung in trees forming a semicircle barricaded in front by wood and brush. An elderly man with a long gray and black beard and bad teeth came out and told us he lived there with two people who'd left. He took the survey, revealed he was only fifty-five, and said, "I don't need to sign up for any services. I'll soon be off the river. I've got an offer to take care of stables and horses. I'll have a room, too."

We thanked him and moved on. One of our crew said, "I think he's dreaming."

Under the overpass of the Golden State Highway we saw an elaborate albeit messy campsite. A tent rested near one of the giant concrete abutments of the bridge, and furniture, pots, pans, clothes, a painting, a pop-up awning, and garbage littered the area in quantities sufficient to fill an average home.

"Kern County," we called. "Here for the census. We have cigarettes and other gifts. Just need a little information."

Two or three minutes of effort evoked no response, but, as at the camp with a tented bicycle, I sensed life. We moved to the bridge's next abutment which served as a rear wall. Several shopping carts curved to define the frontal boundaries of a home without a roof save the highway above. No one was there. We returned to the property-laden site and resumed our requests. Did we hear something? We did. But did the noise come from inside the tent. We kept asking, and hearing sounds, human sounds, groans, perhaps, and then a voice, a female voice we couldn't understand but sensed was in effect saying, wait, I'm coming. We waited at least five minutes. Eventually, a lady wearing a soiled dress emerged. Her thick brown hair was clean and attractively styled.

"Good morning," said the counselor. "Would you like a cigarette?"

"Sure."

The student had taken over the surveying duties, liberating me to stand with pen and papers to record an epic profusion.

"I've only been homeless six weeks," she said. "I used to live in a big house at the country club. I was getting ready to play golf when they kicked me out. My husband, an oil man, lied and said I was on drugs. He called the police and I lost my kid. That was fifteen years ago. Then I had a boyfriend who was a defense attorney. I can't say his name because he's still very prominent. He was no good but not as bad as my next boyfriend. He was a golf instructor but a lazy bastard and rarely gave lessons. I was with him eight years. He was stealing from me the whole time, four-hundred-dollar dresses, anything out of my house he could take, just selling my shit. He was also poisoning me."

As she talked the lady rarely looked at anyone longer than a second, puffing hard on her cigarette, gazing at a world to the west.

"He was a dealer, and he set me up for arrest," she continued. "After I got out of jail I slept in an abandoned house and then got to know people on Union Avenue and slept in prostitution hotels. People there helped me, angels all around, like living in a movie, a trip. I smoked meth but I don't get addicted. I was arrested for drunk driving and public intoxication but my husband set me up. When they hospitalized me, I slashed my wrists."

She only stopped talking to puff. "This isn't my camp. Just because you're homeless doesn't mean you have to live like pigs. Two people had been living here for years. Look how they left everything. I'm going to clean things up. But I won't be here long. I was a body builder and real estate agent. I have two years college. I'm forty-seven. Can I have two more cigarettes?"

The student said, "Here's one more."

We thanked her and headed toward the sand between us and the county vehicle. About a hundred yards from camp, I turned and watched the lady spear papers with a sharp stick and take them about twenty yards west of camp, back and forth she moved, studying the earth, smoking her cigarette.

"How does she keep her hair so clean and well-styled?" I asked the counselor.

"They go to fast food restaurants, regular restaurants, office buildings, places where they can just walk into the bathrooms."

"Why don't these people at the river go to the homeless shelters? They'd be a lot better off."

"A lot of them have warrants and other legal issues," he said.

In a trailside tent a man in his fifties pulled back the canvas. He looked comfortable atop several blankets. His female companion did not answer questions and was visible only to the student surveyor who squatted at the entrance. The man said he'd been homeless nine straight years, was a high school graduate, a veteran of AA and NA meetings, had a history of meth abuse, had battled TB, Hepatitis C, and asthma, and was mentally disabled. He inhaled his cigarette deeply, like most at the river, and spoke with a hoarse voice. He also owned one of the cutest little dogs I've seen.

"What kind of dog is that?" I asked.

"Pomeranian-Chihuahua."

"What percentage of each?"

"Fifty-fifty."

In a little while the man got on his bicycle and rode down the trail, cuddling his little brown dog.

At the start of lunch break, relaxing in a downtown coffee house appreciated for its cookies, artwork, and mellow vibe, we agreed to meet back at The Mission in forty-five minutes. After being dropped there to retrieve my car, I decided to drive home to get more sunscreen. A morning of winter sun had broiled my pale skin, and my back hurt after hiking several miles over difficult terrain. Again I wondered how tough on body and soul it must be to live without a home when it's hot, when it's cold, rainy, or dusty, and it's always dusty along the dry Kern River.

Covered with cream and sated by warm food, I resumed my duties while praying for quitting time, supposedly two p.m. The middle-aged counselor, though not much younger than I, seemed to have more energy in reserve, and his vision remained perhaps too acute. "There's a tent. See that? Are you up for it?"

"Okay," we said. The photographer had excused himself to go to his regular job.

Grinding through soft dirt and sand, and pushing past bushes, reeds, and gnarly trees, we arrived at a campsite featuring a tent in the middle of bushes and dead branches. A baby stroller and lawn chair lounged amid a lot of trash. No one to interview here. We hiked, like a dry version of Humphrey Bogart pulling Katherine Hepburn in *The African Queen* through a swamp. Bogey got leeches. We just got hot and dirty. The counselor, almost as fair as I, asked if his face was red. I said, "Yes." The graduate student, a lad of twenty-five, was unburned and no doubt fresh traveling on youthful legs. I checked my cell phone clock again: about noon, seven hours after our work day began. Empty campsites slowed time on the river. We saw another tent.

"Let me do this one," I said. "Hello, Kern County. Anybody home? We have water, shampoo, toothpaste, and soap for you."

"I can use all those things."

A very slender man emerged. I thought he was sixty or more. During the survey he said he was forty-four.

"Have you had diabetes?"

"I don't know, but I think I have it. Both my parents did."

"You should go to the doctor."

"I don't go to doctors."

"Can we use your name and contact you if you're eligible for more benefits?"

"Yes."

"Please sign here and write your cell phone number or email address."

"I don't have those. I stay to myself."

He handed me the survey, turned, and walked back to his tent in dry bushes.

Homeless Bike Ride

Really, I recommend you come and live in Santee. It's less than twenty miles from San Diego and the beach and not too hot and never real cold and there are pretty brown hills around us and the crime rate's low and I think you'll like it here. Housing's not that expensive compared to most places in this area. I can get you a decent home for less than four hundred grand. If your budget's a little tight, I'll find you a one-bedroom condominium for about one-seventy-five. Sometimes, when jogging on the trail under the Route 52 bridge, I ask myself what it would've taken to get Stephen Hissom a roof over his head. Ordinarily, I might not think about that but can't help it since for a year and a half he lived in a tent in the brush not far from the trail where I run to keep fit and fired up to make lots of sales. I don't know if I ever saw Stephen but I've seen plenty of homeless who stay in this area.

It's a little eerie, what happened, so I never run there at night anymore. Stephen Hissom, age fifty-five, was riding a bicycle, one of his few possessions, with a fellow transient, Edward Allen, about twenty minutes after five p.m. on a late November Saturday last year and it was pretty dark when they encountered six kids. I shouldn't say kids, the three guys were nineteen and two of the three girlfriends were eighteen, the youngest sixteen. I understand that generations of young adults have forever battled their parents, but the last thirty years or so kids have gotten much worse. When I was nineteen and in a pristine area with my girlfriend and buddies and their girlfriends, we didn't battle homeless people, we didn't bother anyone. We passed the brews and joints before jumping into the bushes.

Tyler Dare, Danny Swan, and Brian Kish craved different activities. Dare had just served five months for vehicle theft and Swan was arrested for the same crime but charges against him were dropped. Kish was on probation for misdemeanor burglary a few months earlier. They must've been feeling tough and their girlfriends like badasses. Their lawyers will concoct some ridiculous tales of self-defense, lecturing the jurors how two worn out, middle-aged transients attacked six innocent youths who fought like heck to save themselves. Mind you, this nonsense hasn't been presented yet. But it will be. Wait for the trial. In the preliminary hearing the judge ruled that all five – including Cassidy Rowin and Sarah Baillee, but not the youngest girl, whose charges were dismissed – will be tried as adults. What is the charge?

Edward Allen may not be a reliable witness since he had just gotten out of prison for assault. The physical evidence is likely to be critical and sufficient to convict. Regardless of who first spoke unpleasantly about right of way on the bike and jogging trail, the teenagers attacked Allen – Dare and Swan were most aggressive – and knocked him down, kicked and stomped him, and Stephen Hissom, who could have ridden safely away, turned around and tried to help his friend. The attackers left Allen helpless on the trail and, spurred by the cowardly rage of a mob, battered, stomped, kicked, pounded, and otherwise beat the life out of Hissom. The five tough teenagers should therefore be charged with murder and serve fifteen years to life in prison.

I imagine prosecutors are trying to make deals with the girls, who Allen said shouted at their boyfriends to throw beer bottles at him as he was being trounced, and will offer dramatically reduced sentences in order to go after Tyler Dare and Danny Swan, who probably won't be released from confinement until they've got some gray hair. Brian Kish, I suppose, will serve a little less time.

The relatives of Stephen Hissom are asking for privacy and say they'll learn the story of this crime along with everyone else. There is an important story the family could share at any time. Why was Stephen Hissom living in a tent in the brush near a trail in a suburban area? Had he graduated from high school? What was his work history? Did he have mental health issues and alcohol or drug problems? Was he estranged from the family? Had the family tried to help him? Those questions really aren't part of the trial. They're questions that if answered could explain why there needs to be a trial.

Notes: A year and a half after the attack, Danny Swan and Tyler Dare pleaded guilty to voluntary manslaughter and the judge respectively sentenced them to twelve and fourteen years in prison. Brish

Kish got four years for assault. The two young adult women received three-year sentences for voluntary manslaughter.

Discussing the Homeless

I'm Jeff, a police officer and unit commander eating pot luck in the community room of a middle-class neighborhood where residents must be fifty-five and most are a lot older. After lunch, I walk in front and, speaking without a microphone, ask if everyone can hear me. They can. I'm sure they also notice my beige shirt is more like that of a civilian than a cop, making me less threatening to the homeless, but I'm still equipped with a pistol, a taser, a radio, handcuffs, and plenty more.

There are always rumors, I say. All cities hear others are shipping their homeless to them. It's not true. But if someone is stranded here and wants to return home, we have funds for that. We arrest quite a few people in the mountains east of Bakersfield, bring them to jail here, and when we release them in a day or two they become homeless here.

People who don't have money or shelter flock where the money is – gas stations and stores. Panhandling makes many of them a hundred to a hundred fifty a day, more than minimum wage. They often live in Oildale and ride their bicycles or take the bus to Rosedale. When we ask them why they're here, they say they can't make any money in a poor place like Oildale. We can't cite them anymore if they're panhandling on sidewalks and streets. But if they're trespassing in parking lots or private property, in and around your homes and offices, we can get involved if the owners will go to court and testify. Many don't want to do that. They should, though. Trespassing is likely to continue unless homeowners and supervisors write letters requesting no trespass orders.

The homeless know we're out there to help them, but if they break the law, things like theft and vandalism, we'll arrest them. Your neighborhood here is very inviting to the homeless. You have a lot of carports and external storage sheds. They're easy targets. Be careful about poor lighting and shrubs that are too high. At my house I've got all the shrubs cut back and a security system that rings the doorbell anytime someone steps onto my property. Eleven officers work in my unit throughout the community and at various times. We stop lots of men, and some women, too, who're pushing shopping carts. Sometimes the carts are full of stolen property. It's usually stuff they got out of dumpsters or found in public places. In order to arrest them for having a shopping cart, the cart's got to have identifying markers, like the name of a market. Otherwise, we can't do anything.

The best thing is to help people obtain housing vouchers. The process usually takes about nine months. They just need a driver's license or social security number or birth certificate. Then they have a chance to get long term housing. They need to find landlords who accept Section 8 housing. At this point, though, all their creditors start finding them and billing them. For society, it's good to help the homeless find places to live. It costs fifteen thousand less if they're off the street. That means less police work and fewer medical bills for the homeless. Salt Lake City's spent a lot of money on housing for the homeless and had good results. We need more of that in California. Homeless shelters are helpful, but they're often full. And people can't take their dogs into the shelters so some stay on the streets. Quite a few become squatters in vacant houses. The owner has the right to tell them to leave. But let us do that. Never confront them. You don't know their mental state, their narcotic state, or if they're armed. And make sure never to give them a deadline to leave or it's an oral contract that has to be settled in court.

Eliminate Homelessness

A nation as wealthy as the United States cannot justify having a single homeless person, and it's unconscionable millions have to sleep in streets, alleys, parks, and by rivers. In Bakersfield about one thousand homeless were recently counted. Many more were not. Lower the defense budget a little, cut waste in other bloated departments, and build modest apartment units – perhaps four hundred square feet apiece – for every homeless person in the country. Let's say there are two million people without shelter today. Multiply that by about a hundred dollars a square foot to build an apartment, forty grand per apartment, and the total is a reasonable eighty billion dollars. What are you doing with the family treasure, politicians and governmental bureaucrats? Cut twenty billion a year from defense and other spend-thrifts. It's a modest price to eliminate suffering.

RESTLESS

Gypsies in Madrid

On a summer morning in Madrid, en route to the sumptuous Prado National Museum, I told the taxi driver that the day before I'd visited and been shocked by the harsh industrial neighborhood Villaverde where around the clock provocatively dressed women stand on streets, waiting to rent their bodies.

"I know a place a thousand times worse than that," he said.

"You're kidding."

"No, Valdemingomez is the most tragic place I've ever seen. Gypsies live there."

"How far is it?" I asked.

"Just ten or fifteen minutes."

"Let's go."

A short time later, as he pulled off the freeway and moved toward Valdemingomez, the driver, Fernando, locked all four doors and said, "I'm scared."

I opened my notebook, placed it in my lap, and pulled out a pen.

"It'll be a little dangerous because the Gypsies sell so many drugs: heroin, cocaine, hash, marijuana, LSD, ecstasy."

We moved off a smooth paved road onto an old one marred by many holes. Garbage and mud puddles rotted next to the road in front of dwellings that should not be called houses; they were shacks with cardboard or flimsy wood roofs, and some had corrugated gates that used to be roofs, leading into yards behind graffiti-blighted walls. About a quarter of the lots bore piles of rubble from destroyed shacks, as if Valdemingomez had been repeatedly bombed.

"Terrible."

"The rats here are big as cats," said Fernando.

"Look," I said, and pointed at a young woman frantically running both hands through her long thick curly hair, as if trying to put out a fire.

"Drug addict, probably a prostitute," said Fernando.

Valdemingomez is defined by a long narrow main street like

a pipeline to hell. As we moved deeper inside, numerous women, generally middle-aged and overweight, ran from their homes and insistently motioned for us to pull over. They seemed to have plenty to sell, but we probably wouldn't have gotten out for interviews even if the police hadn't pulled behind us.

"Get ready, they're going to stop us," Fernando said.

"That's fine. I'll show them my notes."

"They're stopping someone else." Several evident drug consumers had driven in from middle-class Madrid. The one behind us would not be leaving with what he came for.

In contrast to the women, a majority of the men we saw were unnaturally thin, almost skeletal, and had gaunt, unshaven faces. These fellows drove dilapidated cars. Unseen and presumably enterprising residents parked plenty of Mercedes Benzes and BMWs in front of shabby homes boasting satellite dishes.

"About ten years ago the government gathered the Gypsies and brought them here," Fernando said. "Most of the kids don't go to school. As you can see, there's not much garbage collection. It's sad."

For a people enslaved by the Romans, murdered by the Nazis, and shunned in most countries, the Gypsy tragedy continues.

* * *

A few years after visiting Spain and writing the story above, I received this email: "Hello, my name is Roger. I'm twenty-four and from England. I currently live in Madrid. I've been here nearly two years. And I know the people of Valdemingomez. Their stories are very interesting and well worth documenting."

I replied with a list of questions and suggested Roger type the answers. He responded that he preferred to talk, especially on camera, because "there are a few things I want to say and ask." He recommended several complex maneuvers on an advanced cell phone, and by email I confessed, "I just have a basic model for calling and texting."

He asked for my phone number and said, aided by a marvelous app, we could talk "absolutely free." About noon Pacific Time on a Saturday I received a call he made at nine p.m. in Madrid.

"Hello, Tom."

"Roger, great to hear from you."

Adjusting to his British accent, I exchanged a little personal information before discussing my experiences in Valdemingomez, and Roger said, "Tom, is there going to be any money in this?"

"No, Roger, I interview many people and write stories before collecting them in books. I'm a publisher. I take the risks. Money can't be part of this conversation."

"Okay," said the genial fellow, "but we still need a microphone and video camera."

We hung up, and within twenty minutes I'd borrowed a laptop with requisite options and was looking at Roger as he broadcast himself sauntering on a Madrid sidewalk, looking cool under a reddish brown pompadour. Our substantive conversation began at once, but in a few minutes he stopped me, held the camera under his left eye, and said, "Look at my eye, Tom, see that? My right eye, too? The same."

"They're a little dark underneath."

"They were quite black until recently. I was beaten early last Saturday morning."

"Jesus."

"I was attacked in Valdemingomez. I arrived Friday afternoon and foolishly stayed quite late. I had an expensive telephone and was perceived as English with lots of money."

"What were you doing there?"

"Smoking crack and heroin."

"Bad news," I said.

"Indeed, though the drugs go quite well together, crack being an upper and heroin a downer."

"I'm not preaching, but you're going to get killed."

"I was in a drug house and needed a ride out of Valdemingomez as it was about five Saturday morning."

"You'd been smoking crack and heroin all that time?"

"Yes. And I asked a dirty husband and his very skinny wife to help. They spoke English well and had a nice car. They tried to make friends and kept telling me how nice they were. I asked them to take me to the bank to get cash. We returned to Valdemingomez and I bought twenty euros of powdered cocaine."

"Powdered? You said you'd been smoking it."

"I was going to rock it up later. I gave them some cocaine for the ride. The lady went bonkers and wouldn't let me speak. I got out of the car and asked for my lighter. Three times I asked, and they said no. I walked away but he drove up behind me, and both got out of the car. I got the man in a headlock but he bit my hand and I let go. His wife attacked me, and the man rugby tackled both of us. He punched me and they both got on top of me, punching, trying to take my bag.

"A man driving by stopped and asked, 'What's going on?'

"'He's trying to rob us,' they said. The car pulled away. I just couldn't punch and landed very few blows. The man was tough. They took my bag and left. I had a concussion and was vomiting. I stumbled to several houses and asked people to call an ambulance but nobody would.

"Then I staggered out of Valdemingomez and flagged down the police. They didn't want to help. They treated me badly because of the place where I was. I felt very looked down on. Finally, the police called an ambulance. In the hospital I asked to speak to the police but was told to talk to a social worker. She wrote the police address, but that was all."

Roger turned off the video portion of our interview as he arrived at his hotel residence.

I asked, "How long were you in the hospital?"

"Several hours, until (last) Saturday afternoon."

Roger emailed me some photos of himself in the hospital, bearing two black eyes and the look of a thrashed puppy.

"Please delete those," he said. "I don't know why I sent them."

After this vigorous opening act, I told Roger we needed some personal history to illuminate the present.

"I was raised north of London. My father worked for an insurance company and is very well off. He and my mother love each other and were very responsible raising me. But my mother announced she was gay and they got divorced. My father lives in London with his new girlfriend. They're going to have a baby.

"In my teens I was expelled from school twice for smoking

marijuana. I eventually went to college to become a motor vehicle mechanic. They put me in some engineering program I wasn't interested in, so I dropped out and worked in a call center. When I was nineteen I met a woman from Spain. She was twenty-four, tall, and beautiful. We got addicted to crack cocaine and heroin."

"North of London?" I asked.

"Yes. We asked the English government for help but couldn't get a response. We decided to move to Madrid to get away from drugs."

I pointed out that Valdemingomez was a poor place to avoid drugs.

"That's true. My girlfriend straightened up and we separated several months ago. She has our son."

"I think that's appropriate," I said.

"I've also got a six-year old girl with another lady."

"You're a popular rascal."

He laughed.

"I went to Valdemingomez looking for a story," I said. "That's clearly not the case with you."

"I came to buy drugs," he said. "I never sold."

"How much do drugs cost in Valdemingomez?"

"A tenth of a gram of cocaine costs six euros (about seven dollars.) Sometimes I smoke crack, others I smoke heroin, and sometimes they sell the drugs mixed."

"That sounds expensive," I said.

"I was spending twenty to forty euros a day."

"That's two or three hundred dollars a week. How do you finance that?"

"I was working in a call center that deals with companies in England. The English company terminated the contract recently. I'm out of work now but think I've got another job at a call center waiting Monday."

"A call center job didn't pay for all those drugs as well as the cost of living, especially with a child."

"My mother also sends me money."

"Do your parents know you're doing drugs?"

"No."

I asked Roger to tell me about the culture of Valdemingomez.

"It's a crazy place," he said. "I recently saw a man looking at a spot on the main road in the morning, and when I returned that night he was still looking at the same spot."

The road full of pot holes crawls by homes that, from outside, appear quite modest.

"Valdemingomez has been there about twenty years," Roger said. "Very few people are working. All the money – the cars, houses, TVs – comes from drugs. People are building fortresses there, and the police don't do anything. A lot of the houses have gates in front and very strong doors. If a family sells drugs, and it seems most do, it hires a junkie to look out for police in front. He tells people like me when I can go in. He says, 'Puerta,' door in Spanish, and another guy inside opens the door. I walk down a passageway to a courtyard and then into a room with bricks or chairs to sit on. They've always got plenty of crack, heroin, or a mixture."

"You haven't been back since you were beaten and robbed eight days ago, have you?"

"I've been back three times."

"That's crazy. Do you live near there?"

"Now I do. The woman I was renting a room from kicked me out. I understand why. I'd lost my job and then came home bruised like this."

"Do you have a car?"

"In England I had a BMW. Here, I take the bus. My hotel's only a short walk to the bus stop."

"I can't believe you've already been back three times. You're going to get killed."

An uncomfortable feeling encroached, and I asked, "You aren't planning to go there tonight, are you?"

"I want to. I'm thinking about it."

"Do you have any pot?"

"Yes."

"All right. Stay in your hotel room tonight and smoke the pot. Don't go back to Valdemingomez. And I mean never go back. Forget your lousy new job that may happen Monday. Get out of Spain now. There are drugs everywhere, but Madrid isn't working for you."

"I think I'm going back to England very soon. I know I should. I could live with my mother in a cottage in the country. Living with her at my age isn't ideal, but I could chop wood and walk the dog."

Campesinos Protest

In the Mexican state of Veracruz prized for oil and agriculture and beautiful beaches, at four o'clock on a 1992 morning, hundreds of campesinos and their families in three pueblos were shaken awake by rumbling. Some were too startled to move. Others ran out of their wood and cardboard shacks and saw caterpillars grinding toward them and waved at the drivers to stop. The drivers and armed and uniformed escorts motioned and yelled for everyone to clear out, granting campesinos minutes to dress and grab a few belongings before the caterpillars lumbered on to destroy their homes as well as schools and churches. This ended more than a decade of living on "ejidos," public land they had farmed and believed should be theirs forever.

* * *

Last week in Mexico City a private driver from my hotel was guiding me down Paseo de la Reforma, grandest boulevard in the country, indeed one of the most elegant and monument-rich in the world, when the scenery suddenly erupted with large banners that said, "The Senate Doesn't See or Hear Us" and "The Senate Doesn't Notice Us". A man named "Dante Delgado" was blamed. On the other side of the visual protests loomed bleak plastic dwellings anchored by ropes and no higher than three or four feet.

"What's going on?" I asked.

"This is the *Movement of the 400 Pueblos*," said the driver. "Every day they take off their clothes and protest in public."

"You're kidding."

"No, I'm not."

"I want to talk to them."

"Fine. Just ahead, at the *Monumento a la Madre*, they have their main camp. But I'll have to use the public parking lot."

"No problem. I'll pay."

We entered the concrete campground, bordered to the west by

the gigantic stone Madre, and for several minutes walked around, noting the difficulties of living there, before we approached a few men in a group.

"I'm a writer from California," I said. "May I please have an interview?"

In less than a minute they'd summoned their spokesman, an energetic fellow who shook my hand and introduced himself as Jaime Rodriguez Barrientos.

"Who's Dante Delgado?" I asked.

"Dante Delgado was the interim Governor of Veracruz in 1992," said Rodriguez. "He repressed campesinos and is the one who ordered the destruction of our villages – Alamo Temapache, Poza Rica, and Martinez de la Torre. Then he invented charges and jailed three hundred people. Twelve were in jail for seven years and many others from eight months to two years. We struggled for the freedom of our comrades until 2000. Since then we've been fighting for the return of our land."

"Why did Dante Delgado destroy your homes?"

"He represents the interests of the rich and the powerful."

"Is he taking bribes?" I asked.

"We're not saying he takes bribes. But he's certainly our enemy. So are the men who succeeded him as governor – Patricio Chirinos, Miguel Aleman, and Fidel Herrera, who's in office now."

"Why do you believe the land you lived on belonged to you?"

"We had established ourselves there and no wealthy men had a legal right to it. Delgado claims that what he did was legal and the right thing."

"How long have you been here in Mexico City?" I asked.

"Four months."

"Why now?"

"Dante Delgado was out of power after 1995. In this country there's no point in chasing someone with no office. When Dante became a senator last year, we decided to go after him."

Gradually some men from the camp had begun to gather around us and about twenty now watched the interview.

"I hear you guys have been publicly protesting in the nude," I said.

"That's right," said Rodriguez. "And sometimes our wives, too."
Several men laughed.

"What's the purpose of taking off your clothes in public?"

"By protesting naked we're demonstrating that we lack justice.
Every day we do this from ten a.m. to two p.m. We go all over, to the
Zocalo, the Palacio de Belles Artes, to the Senate of the Republic, to
Dante Delgado's office, and other places."

"Aren't you concerned about losing public support by being naked
in public?"

"Only three or four out of a hundred are offended."

"What about the police? Don't they do anything about the nudity
or camping here?"

"No. No problema," Rodriguez said, and handed me a photo. "I
want you to have this."

I thanked him and examined four naked men, two standing at
attention and two playing drums. "You guys are in good shape."

"Of course, we're campesinos," declared a man from the group.

"How long will you stay here?" I asked.

"Until we get a response," Rodriguez said. "Until the senate
demonstrates it understands the need to investigate Dante Delgado.
He's a coward. He hid from an interviewer from TV Azteca, but he
can't hide from us. We're going to chase him the rest of his life."

I extended my hand toward plastic huts stretched much too low
to stand in.

"Are you guys, and in many cases your wives and children, comfortable here?"

From the group a young man said, "When it rains hard at night,
the water comes in under the plastic. We have to sleep sitting up,
and that's hard."

"Where do you go to the bathroom?"

"We use the gas station's bathroom across the street," said
Rodriguez. "It costs two pesos (about twenty cents) each time."

"Expensive," I said. "And food, all the other things. How do you
support yourselves?"

"We get donations, usually one or two pesos, but sometimes people
give us a lot more." (My driver and another Mexico City resident told

me they believe the opposition PRD party is also providing support. Its leader, Andres Manuel Lopez Obrador, lost a close and disputed presidential election in 2006 to Felipe Calderon.)

As I spoke to the men, several women were dunking clothes in buckets of water and scrubbing garments on stones at the base of the *Monumento a la Madre*. Two men, glistening brown in the sun, stood nearby, washing themselves with rags also dipped in buckets. All water for three hundred protestors comes from a single tap.

"I don't know how long you can last under these conditions," I said.

"Bathing like that is no problem," said a muscular man from the photo. "Like typical campesinos we bathed in arroyos. We're living better here than in Veracruz. Here we only have one family in each place. In Veracruz we had four families in one-room casitas of wood and cardboard."

Mexican Teachers Protest

A few blocks from the campesinos, at the *Monumento de la Revolución*, three thousand teachers were protesting. The following day, with another driver from my hotel, I entered an impressive campground that featured new tarps pulled together high and wide enough to walk under and stretch out. I identified myself and requested an interview. Shortly, Alvarez Juarez was brought forth, and he and three other teachers, one a woman, offered the driver and me comfortable chairs in a patio-like area beneath canvas stretched between two residences.

"What is your position?" I asked.

"I'm the National Coordinator of Education Workers from Guerrero," said Juarez, a polite but serious man. "I've taught elementary school thirty years in Acapulco."

"What are the issues you're most concerned about?"

"We're here because of the new law about our pension fund. We used to pay three and a half percent, now the government says we have to pay ten point six."

"I'm a teacher in California, and we pay eight percent and have very good benefits," I said. "You have to put in more than three and a half to get the benefits you need."

"We aren't going to get anything. They're going to rob us."

"Who are they?"

"President Felipe Calderon and Ester Gordillo, leader of the National Education Workers' Union, and the politicians and business interests they represent. They claim they want to increase pension benefits for our children and our retirement benefits and to improve hospitals and health care, but we know they really want more money to pay their debts to the International Monetary Fund and the World Bank."

At that moment I knew little about Ester Gordillo and the teacher's union in Mexico, and thought the eternal cry of corruption was exaggerated. A little reading, however, revealed that Gordillo's predecessor, Carlos Jonguitud, "was accused of masterminding the assassination of at least one hundred fifty dissident teachers, primarily in the southern states of Oaxaca and Chiapas." Gordillo by comparison is a model of moderation, having only "been implicated in the deaths of several teachers that were struggling to democratize the National Education Workers' Union."

The problem is systemic rather than personal. Gordillo is merely the latest head of a union, like most in Mexico, that has long abused its members. According to Colin Brayton of WorldPress.com, recent surveys show that ninety-eight percent of Mexican teachers "believe the main priority of their leadership is to enrich themselves and hold on to power... and eighty-seven percent believe that their dues are held onto by the leadership and used to buy support... and only one percent of (union) members consider that their leadership has a genuine commitment to education."

"The government has been closed and hasn't given any response to our concerns," Juarez continued. "The government says it's a good law and we need to accept it. We're going to keep trying to change the law. We have marches, protests, lots of activities. On July twenty-sixth we're going to march at the United States Embassy."

"Why the U.S. Embassy?" I asked.

"To protest the war in Iraq and the arrogant treatment of people in Latin America."

Unlike the dour Juarez, his colleague next to me was enjoying the interview, and said, "We know Americans think Mexicans are sucking their thumbs. But we know what's going on. We have eyes. That's why we don't like your president, Adolf Bush."

"I don't care for Bush, either," I said. "But I guarantee he's a long way from being Adolf. And, by the way, I wrote a book about Adolf called *Hitler Here*, so I know."

"Just remember, we Mexicans aren't sucking our thumbs," said the colleague.

Juarez leaned forward and handed me a tabloid titled "Program of Activities" with daily schedules comparable to boot camp. Every day starts at six a.m. with bathing then community cleaning, breakfast, two hours of conferences in an auditorium followed, in different places, by lectures, another hour in the auditorium then more meetings, lunch at three p.m., workshops, cultural events in the auditorium, an hour for dinner at nine p.m., and two hours of free time ending at midnight when most are already in bed, preparing for the next early wakeup.

"Where do you guys, and the ladies and kids I see around here, go to the bathroom?" I ask.

"We use the public bathroom across the street. It costs three pesos each time and five to bathe."

"How are you supporting yourselves?"

The Secretary of Public Education is still paying our teachers' salaries, about three thousand pesos every fifteen days, six thousand a month."

"That's about six hundred dollars a month," I said. "Is that sufficient?"

"It's not sufficient even when we're just maintaining our homes. Now we're maintaining them as well as our community here."

"How long are you prepared to stay?"

"We've been here three months and are prepared to stay as long as necessary."

"Are you going to march naked in public?"

"We're not going to undress, unless we get desperate," said a still unsmiling Juarez.

Notes: Two people mentioned above have been in the news. Manuel Andres Lopez Obrador was elected president of Mexico in 2018, and former leader of the teacher's union Elba Ester Gordillo, following several years of imprisonment on charges of embezzling about a hundred billion dollars, was released from prison and then house arrest and absolved of all charges, for which Mexican authorities never put her on trial.

East Aguascalientes

Aren't those great houses behind guarded gates north of Aguascalientes. I'll never live there, of course, but I dream about marble and tile under high ceilings of Nissan executives, and doctors and businessmen, and smaller large homes of others. My place in the Los Pericos neighborhood east of town is different. It seems drier out here where few trees and plants grow. We can't worry about that. We've got to eat and get through hot summers and cold winters. In regular houses you may not worry so much about the weather, but the roof over our heads is thin aluminum held down by rocks in each corner and in the middle of each side. Walls are stones and aluminum, and a tarp serves as the front and only door. I wish we had plumbing but instead step across a dirt road, which chokes us when cars drive by, and into sharp brown weeds and then go around back and wash up at the water faucet. We had a hose before someone stole it.

I'd love to clean those big houses but it takes more than an hour to walk and ride the bus north, and I know they wouldn't think I look right, anyway. When there's work I clean small offices downtown. I don't know what my husband does but he used to drink a lot. Then he left. My oldest son of three boys and four girls is doing pretty well as a taxi driver. He and his family live near here in a small house with plumbing and a fenced yard guarded by two big dogs.

Sometimes he picks me up, and the three kids still at home, and drives us to the beautiful mall in the north. Our favorite luxury store is Sears. We can't afford the fabulous products but enjoy being near them. Imagine, a pair of jeans for a hundred twenty dollars. If they tear holes in the knees, the jeans cost two hundred fifty, more than I make a month. People with a little more money can buy clothes on credit over six or eighteen months. Sears also has a lot of beautiful furniture. My favorite is the sofa, corner, and love seat that go together and cost six thousand six hundred dollars. I'm always embarrassed when the clerks come over. They can't help me, and I wonder if they actually buy the stuff they sell.

Streets of Mexico City

I'm very comfortable curled up my knees on the sidewalk and the rest of me on an old blanket in front of the door of a little food store closed today. I sleep here and other spots during the day and have many other places to sleep at night. My favorite is the back of a truck with a roof. It belongs to a friend. I guess he isn't really a friend. I don't have any friends. But many people are friendly. Today the lady who owns the little store brings me two ham sandwiches and a big plastic glass of milk. I wave to her and her family and smile open a mouth missing all but a few teeth.

I'm very happy and don't mind sleeping in alleys or under trees, bridges, and freeways. They're my home. As an adult I've rarely had any other. I'm fifty-nine years old but look seventy and ill. That doesn't matter. Neither do most other things. In the streets I'm free.

As a very young man I didn't much like living with my mother. I think she expected me to make more money and get married. I tried to earn a living but couldn't despite shining lots of shoes. Look. I've still got my old wood shoeshine box. I don't shine many shoes anymore, though. I don't feel well enough. Most of the time I have to rest. My mother knew I was slow. But she could only help while she lived because she rented and when she died I was on the streets the first time. After I got a few teeth knocked out my aunt took me in but was very critical so I left.

Sometimes I got a little worn out on the streets and went to those places for the homeless. I never stayed long. They always said get up now, eat this, go look for a job, be back by this time, go to bed now. I was anxious to get back to my home under the sky. I didn't need much. I never drank or used drugs. I never wanted them. I just wanted to lie down and rest. Sometimes pretty women told me they wanted to lie down with me. That made me happy. But when I woke up my money was always gone.

Now I'm eating my second ham sandwich. My gums are hard and I really don't need the teeth I have. I don't need much except the clothes I'm wearing and my blanket and an old bag with a few supplies including insulin for diabetes and of course my shoeshine box. I don't need to go more than several kilometers from this spot and don't think I ever have. I don't need to know who the president is or even what is a president. Those things don't concern me. I'm free in the streets of Mexico City.

Alive in Manila

There aren't any squatters among a million deceased residents in vast Manila North Cemetery. If my family doesn't pay the lease every five years, someone living among the headstones and colorful tombs will earn three bucks to dig me up for cremation. That's reasonable work. Six thousand poor people need a little food and shelter more than a dead man needs a coffin and space. Coming from a wealthy family, I never considered these matters until I drove too fast and got moved here.

I feel like I'm part of the community and don't say much when people sell drugs and fight. I'm all right as long as they don't bother me. It does worry me, though, when the Philippine National Police charge in here and start shooting. Sometimes the tough guys really do shoot first but often it's the police. Quite a few people live next to or over modest graves of sons who died without due process. Parents say they feel better being close and able to talk to departed sons and are comforted by the prospect of someday joining them.

Meanwhile, residents above ground build headstones and coffins and sell flowers and scramble other ways trying to get some informal schooling for their children who chase each other around the graves and, when they're a little older, play spirited basketball games on dirt courts. When the weather's unbearably hot and humid or rain never stops or typhoons strike, it's tough on the living but not so bad for the dead.

ON THE MOVE

Wealth

fertile
farms
make
billions
for owners
and paupers
of pickers
subject to
deportation

Mexico to Tucson on Foot

The drive from Acapulco to Cuanacaxtitlán takes two to three hours depending how fast you want to negotiate rocky roads getting rougher deep into the state of Guerrero. The trip prepares you for what you will find: a village locked in a time long ago and shrouded in heat and humidity and neglect. Most of the world, even most of Mexico, does not know much about Cuanacaxtitlán and the indigenous people there. And they do not want to know. Juan can tell you why. Life there does not accommodate comfort or happiness.

Like many in the region, Juan was a campesino, and he and his coworkers always planted by hand. Corn and beans grew in the hills, and peanuts on the plain, and he walked with an iron bar, pounding holes in resistant ground, and with the other hand retrieved seeds from a can and placed them in every hole. Harvesting was even more difficult than planting, and during their two one-hour breaks the campesinos not only rested but diligently sharpened their machetes and hoes. Peanuts were the toughest to get. Plants crouched low to the ground and the peanuts grew six inches underground. With his hoe Juan hammered crevices, which when viewed from above look like bicycle spokes leading away from each plant. Now the plants could be pulled out and roughly two kilos of peanuts per plant picked and tossed into big boxes. Corn was taken one ear at a time, one leading to another to thousands to eternity. Frijoles were the least difficult to acquire; plants graciously died at harvest time so they could readily be uprooted and placed on plastic then hammered with long wooden sticks.

Prices for the crops were low, wages lower, and Juan and his wife, Silvia, and their eight children lived in a house with two small rooms: the youngest kids slept with their parents and the rest stayed in the other room. Their oldest daughter escaped to the United States at age sixteen. A couple of years later Juan concluded local farming would never lead anywhere nor could he regularly use construction skills he'd also learned. There was only one life-changing course: go North to the land of opportunity, and work and try to save to build a decent house back home.

In spring Juan and Silvia left their seven remaining children with relatives before flying from Acapulco to Hermosillo, Sonora, and then paid sixty dollars to be driven close to the border in a village called Altar. There they rendezvoused with their coyote, a boy of sixteen who'd been recommended by friends. The youth had enthusiastically come from California to Altar; Juan and Silvia and four other adults from their town – three men and a woman – each paid him twelve hundred dollars. He told them which supplies to acquire. The best food would be dry beans, tortillas, bread, sardines and salsa. Everyone would take as much water as could be carried. Each man ran ropes through the handles of five one-gallon plastic water bottles and strapped them over his shoulders; the women did so with four bottles. They all had hats, jackets, sweaters, and tennis shoes. It was eight p.m., time to cross the border.

"I wonder what could happen," Juan thought.

They began to walk. It was dark in the desert and usually quiet except when coyotes howled.

"Don't worry about them," said the one with two legs. "And mountain lions, they won't attack this many people. But watch out for snakes."

"We won't be able to see the snakes," said Juan.

"You can't see the spiders, either."

All night they walked, progressively more worried about the future than current confrontations with nature. In the morning the desert sun shone hot early, and they foraged for branches broken by the wind and found enough to cover themselves in the sand where they slept all day. As darkness came they resumed walking, and walked all night and when the second day began they did not stop. They tried to preserve their energy and supplies, resting twenty minutes every two hours and limiting what they ate and drank. But resources were dissipating, they had to keep moving. Juan was thinking about his daughter. Just before he departed, she'd left a message with a rare relative who had a phone: her boyfriend was a methamphetamine addict and crazy most of the time and beating her and taking her money from the government and ignoring their baby daughter. Juan and Silvia had to get to the

United States. Actually, they were already in the great land, but only technically, heading somewhere in the desert.

They walked hard all the third night. In fact, they were moving slower but using more energy. Most people don't train for this. Only the fresh young coyote could've walked much faster.

"You know where we are?" Juan asked.

"Of course."

He was already a pro who didn't bother with a compass. His eyes and ears told him everything.

"We're out of food and water's low," said Juan.

"No problem. I know a ranch."

Through the sand and brush and over dunes and around cactus and other rough spots he guided them. They were surely going the right way: there on the horizon stood cows, beautiful awkward cows, standing in perpetual bovine stupor as the group now walked harder toward them. The people wanted to run. They would have if they could. They walked fast enough. Now they were there, next to cows ignoring them as they stuck thirsty human heads into troughs. Dirtiest water they'd ever had, and by far the best. They drank till wet all over, then filled a few empty plastic bottles they still carried. It was about half past eight when they resumed walking. Everything was better now.

"Look," the coyote soon said, softly.

All seven eased down – then at once, guided by a spontaneous signal wrought by hunger, they rose and fired their rocks. Six missed the target. One, thrown by a strong-armed fellow from Cuanacaxtitlán, nailed a jackrabbit in the head. They converged, making sure he wasn't just stunned and getting ready to dash. He wasn't. They drew knives and skinned and gutted the rabbit and placed it face down and open in a fire for a half-hour.

"Delicious," said Juan. "I'd eaten iguanas in Guerrero; the jackrabbit was even better."

Fortified, they walked with more energy and optimism, and they did so all day. In the afternoon they reached the outskirts of Tucson where the boy told them to wait. In twenty minutes he was back, driving a car that took them to the house of one of his friends. They slept and ate in the house for a bargain of thirty dollars each for all three days. Ultimately, a mini-van arrived. Another friend of the coyote had driven it from Lamont, California, a poor farming community near Bakersfield. Twelve people wedged into the vehicle. Juan and Silvia paid no more since their initial investment was a package deal. New travelers handed over three hundred dollars for the twelve-hour trip to Lamont. One should note that prices for coyote-guided immigration are going up faster than housing costs in California. Today, Juan and Silvia would need three grand apiece for the same array of services.

In Lamont, Juan and Silvia were encouraged. If you're from the United States, you'd probably think many of the houses are tiny and old and crying for paint and repair. When you're from Cuanacaxtitlán, the modest structures seem all right, even surrounded by flat and dreary terrain. Juan and Silvia were more concerned about their daughter, who also lived in the community.

"If you don't leave that guy, you'll always have problems," Juan said.

"I love him," said the daughter.

"If you don't leave him, I'll go back to Mexico."

"Go ahead."

"If you don't leave, I'll call the police."

A week later, rushing to where her parents were staying, she bore a black eye from a punch and bruises and welts all over her body where she'd been hit with a broom and snapped by the cord of an iron.

"Okay," she said.

Now the family is living nine in a small two-bedroom house. The daughter and a kinder boyfriend have a baby boy, and, with the little girl, sleep four in one bedroom. The next three oldest children, a twelve-year old and two teenage boys, followed their parents to the United States. They were led by another coyote. The boys stay in the second bedroom. Juan and Silvia sleep in the living room. During the day the daughter takes care of her children and youngest brother. He does not go to school. Neither do the teenage boys. They are already fieldworkers, like their parents. Juan knows they should be in school but is afraid of inquiries about documents and immigration status. The teenagers may never see another classroom.

Juan and Silvia go to work together five days a week. They each pay seven dollars a day for the ride in a van. They just finished several months of picking oranges for eleven dollars a large box. (They'll soon start harvesting grapes.) Juan could usually fill five boxes a day with oranges, making fifty-five dollars or about seven an hour for eight hours labor. Silvia generally did four boxes, earning roughly five-fifty an hour, well under minimum wage. Of course, their employers reminded them, they weren't paying taxes. That helped. It certainly helped the employers avoid a variety of irksome expenses like fair pay and health care and social security.

If you figure Juan and Silvia have twenty picking days a month, they are each spending one hundred forty dollars for the rides, or between fifteen and twenty percent of their wages. Their little house rents for four hundred fifty a month. There are also the usual gas, electric, phone and food bills. Yet, in an impressive display of dedication and frugality, they're ble to send five hundred dollars a month to their four children who still live with relatives in Cuanacaxtitlán.

"Life is a little better in the United States," said Juan. "But we aren't able to save any money. I still want to build a big house in Mexico someday. Maybe we'll live in it, maybe we'll sell. If I can't bring my other kids here, I'll go back."

Labor Recruitment

Gerardo is a contratista – a labor contractor. He operates in the agriculture-rich Central Valley of California. People like him also lurk in other businesses and states but he loves it here because many owners of huge farms crave cheap labor. Almost year round they need people to pick their oranges, tangerines, tomatoes, kiwis, grapes or carrots, and they certainly are not going to do it nor are their children or friends. And Gerardo won't be doing it, either. He's too smart, too well-connected. He's the guy a supervisor for an agri-business goes to and says, "Hey, we need about forty workers."

"No problem," Gerardo replies. He summons his brother Miguel and sends him south to Guanajuato, Jalisco, Puebla, and other places in Mexico where people have so little they'll listen as he says, "I've got jobs for you. The pay's very good. And I'll take care of your expenses now. Only thirty thousand pesos (about three thousand dollars). When you work, you can pay me back."

Miguel often recruits sixty to eighty men and puts them on buses bound north. When they arrive, Gerardo's carefully-developed contacts cram the workers into dingy motel rooms where they wait for coyotes who charge more than a thousand dollars a head. They are the good part Miguel has told the men about; these coyotes will make it easy; they'll save your lives. Gerardo and Miguel aren't concerned about their personal well-being but know three or four hundred Mexicans a year perish in the desert – a million more are captured – and they won't get paid unless the workers make it to farms in central California.

Gerardo doesn't risk all the capital at once. One of his coyotes orders five to ten workers to buy water and running shoes prior to darting across the border at night. Next morning, elsewhere, another coyote puts four or five people in boxes back of a truck and tries to drive across. Two nights later in another area a coyote leads a group on foot. Gerardo likes his guys waiting here, dashing there, riding somewhere else while others are poised as his experts assess the border. It's too risky now. Okay. Maybe tomorrow. It won't be long. Let's get a couple of dependable teenagers with nice SUVs to drive a few in. Soon all the workers have tried. And Gerardo's nervous waiting for calls. Maybe things won't work out this time. Could be he's paid thousands for nothing. Ultimately, he receives good news. About eighty percent have made it. Compare that, he proudly thinks, to the reported national success rate of one-half to two-thirds.

Many workers are in a new world; for others it's the second, third, fourth time or more. They're picked up by veteran drivers crossing the grotesque desert of southeastern California and relieved when they arrive in the Central Valley, the promised land where Highway 99 leads to Bakersfield, Delano, Tulare, Fresno, Madera, and Merced as well as many surrounding communities.

Gerardo's group arrives near Bakersfield. Twenty or more pay a hundred fifty to two hundred dollars a month to live in a trailer and a similar number stay in a two bedroom house where they vie for one of the few beds, often sharing them or sleeping on ragged sofas or the floor. Sometimes an old sleeping bag can be found. It's vital to rest. Days are long and arduous, beginning before sunrise as vans pick the workers up and head to fields of the fruit in season. The daily ride costs five or six bucks a head. If the passengers complain, Gerardo, in his capacity as foreman, tells them it's a bargain considering they're being driven twenty, thirty, forty miles each way. Besides, how else you going to get there?

They're picking oranges six days a week now, standing on ladders and sticking their faces into insects and branches and leaves with pesticide residue. Endlessly they reach to grasp the next orange. Grab those beautiful ugly things. Grab 'em fast as you can. This job is about production. Workers are paid twelve dollars and fifty cents for each large box filled with oranges. When inexperienced, they can only do about three boxes a day. They have to improve. Their burrito during break costs two dollars, same as the burrito for lunch. Add up expenses for lodging, transportation, food on the job, and food at home – forget all the other stuff – and the total is four to five hundred a month, out of earnings of eight hundred. The remaining three hundred dollars or so go to Gerardo. They still owe him almost three grand, and he's got big time expenses. Don't forget, he says, I had to pay for those coyotes and lots of other stuff.

The workers are young, strong and motivated, and now they're filling six to eight boxes a day. Their cash earnings are way up and so are their payments to Gerardo, who is more diligent accounting their debt than always fully paying for labor. You don't like it, get another job, find another place to stay, Gerardo tells them. That usually ends the discussion. Gerardo's got things under control. But even he can't dominate nature. Workers eventually note that once they could fill a box with oranges from two trees, and that took about an hour. Now the oranges are so sparse they must be picked from sixteen trees to fill a box; that requires two hours. They aren't going to take a fifty percent pay cut, not if they're ever going to get out of debt.

One day thirty workers encircle Gerardo and say: "Either pay us more per box or we won't work."

Gerardo reaches into his jacket, pulls out a gun, and announces: "I'll shoot the first cabrón who tries to leave."

Minutemen on the Border

At this moment about five hundred volunteers for the Minuteman Project are in southern Arizona on a self-assigned, self-righteous, and utterly overwrought mission to "protect" the United States from impoverished Mexicans trying to enter this country on foot to perform hard tasks most Americans would never consider doing. Even the most ardent nationalists understand Mexicans would not come to the United States unless they were virtually assured of being hired by (usually white) employers seeking workers they can pay very little.

If the Minutemen really don't want illegal immigrants to pick fruit and vegetables, and take care of Anglo babies, and clean their houses, then they should themselves perform the aforementioned and other unpleasant duties. Or, if they aren't prepared for that – and evidently they are not – then they should use their zeal for citizen law enforcement to confront countless employers across this nation and compel them to stop hiring those without proper documentation. Step into the farm fields and announce the police have been called. By doing so, the Minutemen would initiate the capture of more illegal immigrants in an hour than they will in a projected one month in Arizona. But they aren't going to do that, either, are they?

What the Minutemen want most is attention, and they're getting some, but fate has dealt them a bad inaugural week to compete for headlines: the Pope died, baseball season opened, Saul Bellow passed away, and Peter Jennings was diagnosed with lung cancer. The volunteer sentinels, who disrupt the real United States Border Patrol by setting off underground sensors and tramping more footprints in the sand, probably won't make much news unless someone – one of them or the other guys – is killed or wounded. The Minutemen swear that won't happen. They're actually a "neighborhood watch group along our border … that has no affiliation with separatists, racists, or supremacy groups." Theirs "is not a call to arms but a call to voices seeking a peaceful and respectable resolve to the chaotic neglect" by politicians at all levels in "applying U.S. immigration law."

They want everyone to know this "nation is governed by the rule of law," and they're sacrificing the "comforts of a cozy home" so they can do something to prevent their homeland from being "devoured and plundered by the menace of tens of millions of invading illegal aliens." If this isn't stopped, the Minutemen warn, "future generations will inherit a tangle of rancorous, unassimilated, squabbling cultures with no common bond to hold them together" which will lead to a "certain guarantee of the death of this nation as a harmonious melting pot." Thus, people "will write about how a lax America ... (sank) into a quagmire of mutual acrimony among various sub-nations that will comprise the new self-destructing America."

Exhale, and note that the Minutemen have many more warnings but those above should suffice to convince everyone they are genuinely tortured by the current and future condition of the United States. Sincere people deserve a serious response. And I hereby assure the Minutemen – the vacationing vigilantes, not the Patriots who battled King George's well-trained Red Coats – that the apocalypse is not upon us. I am qualified to offer such a guarantee. For many years I taught English as a Second Language for adults, eighty percent of whom are from Mexico. I know the people, and they're unequivocally not ruining this country; they're building it with their hands and backs and hearts, the way immigrants always have. They're also infusing their new land with energy and optimism. Often, I ask students if they miss Mexico, and most say not much. No disrespect to their native land, they simply love the opportunities and way of life here.

The primary issue, then, is not security but the rule of law. Immigration standards are indeed being violated, but not because the United States is indifferent. Last year, in fact, twenty thousand Border Patrol agents arrested more than a million illegal entrants. That's impressive intervention, but for every person seized two got through. Do the political and economic rulers of the United States consider that an invasion? Of course not. If they did, they'd put a lot more agents or soldiers along the two-thousand mile border with Mexico.

Let's further clarify matters by stating what leaders of the United States and Mexico have long known, and what anyone with access to a map should also understand: the American Southwest is destined to be inhabited by millions more people of Hispanic origin. This is a mandate of geopolitics and history; the wealthier nation, which won the Mexican-American War and most desirable territory, is an inexorable magnet for those desperate for economic betterment. Their hot and often dangerous journeys on foot are comparable to the perilous voyages long ago from Europe. And Mexican immigrants, like their European predecessors, will not cease coming in great numbers until opportunities improve at home.

Why Immigrants Work Here

Those who vigorously oppose the presence of undocumented workers in the United States offer many reasons for their conviction. One of the most prominent is "illegal aliens" take jobs that otherwise would be filled by U.S. citizens. Do you know anyone who'd want this job? Last week in a vineyard north of Bakersfield, twenty-three Spanish-speaking women were picking grapes when a large truck began spraying weed-killing poison on an adjacent field of oranges. A strange odor enveloped the women but they kept working until feeling "dizzy and nauseated," according to the *Bakersfield Californian*. They ran to the opposite end of the field where tears filled burning eyes, and four women went into convulsions. Nine-one-one was called and firefighters rushed in, put up blinds for privacy, instructed the women to strip to their underwear, and helped hose them off before they were taken to the hospital. No one died. And all were released that day.

Some of the ladies are no doubt back at work. Perhaps all have returned. But don't worry. There are still plenty of openings, and U.S. citizens can get these low-paying jobs anytime: you won't need an education or training or even identification. You just have to bend over and break your backs in the heat and cold and wind and dust as you inhale pesticides, which are always there. In Kern County they officially sicken about a hundred workers a year. Many more are also devoured, slowly and at first imperceptibly, by chronic exposure to poison.

How often do you see farm workers closer than driving by in your climate-controlled cars? I had some in my English as a Second Language class at night. Most of their coworkers never will make it to school. They're too tired. Those who come often arrive late from the fields and leave early so they can sleep a little and rise before dawn. Almost all have very little education; some have never attended school. Few will ever learn English well. It's going to be difficult to escape the fields. Their children will be the ones to do that.

Notes: After first writing about the contributions and difficulties of illegal immigration, readers deluged me with emails. Overwhelmingly, the letter writers denounced those who have broken the law in order to work here. Regarding the poisoned farmworkers, one of my rare letter-writing supporters sent me this ironic note: "I really hope the INS investigated the immigration status of these ladies because they certainly are taking jobs away from hardworking Americans."

Grower in the Fields

Here in the Year of our Lord 1965 I tell you I'm proud to be a grower in the fertile Central Valley of the Golden State and a generous man trying to help poor Mexicans and Filipinos and others pursue the American Dream. That's why I'm so damned angry at their betrayal. They're striking and telling reporters from all over that growers aren't paying and treating them right. That just isn't true. Damn right I accept their challenge to go out and prove my case.

First off, at five a.m., I drive my pickup truck into one of the housing camps. These are fine structures with wood walls and sealed roofs that don't leak and little chimneys connected to stoves to keep the places warm and fresh inside. There's no indoor plumbing but they have pumps nearby and a couple of outhouses.

"Do you want to live in one of those places?" they ask.

"I've already got a home."

"Big, heated, and air conditioned."

"That's right. Three generations of my family worked for that," I say.

"And three generations of other families worked to make you rich."

"They worked here because I offered the best jobs they could get."

"You want to live here or not?" asks a worker.

"I'll stay awhile, but not forever."

"Wonderful," he says. "Now it's time to go to work. You aren't afraid of work, are you?"

"I've been working twelve-hour days all my life."

"Here's your hoe."

"I'll get a longer one in my truck."

"No, you'll use the same short-handle hoe as everyone else, working close to the ground so we see if you stop working a second and stand to ease your back.

"My back's fine."

"You haven't stooped yet."

I don't say anything but it's hot as hell by nine a.m. and I'm sweating like a hog. "How 'bout some water?"

Twenty people use the same cup to drink warm water before it finally gets to me, and I say, "I want my own damn cup and cold water."

"So do we. Why don't we have them?"

"Okay, let me write that down."

They insist I sign my promise for individual cups and cold water. Back at work I get dizzy and start to sneeze, then come the coughs. "You tryin' to gas me?"

"We thought you loved pesticides."

"Never ordered this much."

"Who did?"

"I'll look into it."

"Write that down."

I do, and say, "How 'bout a handkerchief as a gas mask."

"Here, se**ñor,**" says a lady.

"Thanks."

"One dollar."

"Pretty steep."

"About what I make an hour."

I hand her a buck and am tempted to tell her I've got a few million more.

"We should receive at least the minimum wage," they say.

"I can't afford that."

"That's not true and a big reason we're on strike."

I'm ready to slug people calling me a liar but need to take a dump. I peed earlier but that was easy. Try finding a private place, dropping your drawers, and squatting in some hot and dusty part of hell. "Hey, anybody got some toilet paper?"

They laugh, and I almost do too.

"Sure," says a man. He walks over, looking the other way and holding his nose, and hands me a roll.

"Thanks a lot."

"One dollar."

"Fine, soon as I finish."

"Lucky you're not a woman," he says.

"So are you."

"We need outhouses equipped with toilet paper and regularly cleaned."

"Fine," I say.

In a few minutes a man says, "Sign here."

I do, and we get back to work, bending, squatting, kneeling, picking, and hoeing. My damn back's aching but I'm not going to say anything. It seems like a week before quitting time arrives. "Okay, folks, see you tomorrow."

"We'll see you tonight, in the camp," they say.

"I better get home."

"Home's in the camp."

It's hotter in the damn house than outside and there's no TV or stereo or books or electricity or anything to do but lie down, take off my clothes, and use my stinking shirt to rub sweat off myself. Later that afternoon I pay a guy two bucks to bring me smelly tacos, bad beans, and warm water. In the morning I'm so sore I barely make it out of bed and stumble outside to say, "Can't work today, folks, damn back's acting up."

"You've only used the short-hoe one day," they say. "We've used it for years."

"We'll get you some regular hoes."

"Sign that."

I do.

"Get me a doctor."

"You don't have health insurance."

"I sure do."

"Not out here."

"I got money."

"Not out here."

"Let's pretend you don't have any more work for me, and I'll move on," I say.

"You don't have unemployment insurance. In the same situation as you, we'd have to work."

"I own the damn place."

"Yes, and we expect you to sign a contract promising us minimum wages and insurance and housing with indoor plumbing."

"You know I can't do that."

"Why not?"

"I'll have to talk to the other growers."

"When?" they ask.

"Right away."

Two guys, one holding each of my arms, help me walk to my pickup and the guy on my left arm helps me get in.

"Adios," I say.

Delano Grape Strike

As a little boy at school in the Philippines we every morning pledged allegiance to the United States flag and "liberty and justice for all." I couldn't go to school long – had to work in the fields to help my parents support eleven kids – but for several years got more excited every time I made the pledge, and heard stories of great wealth in our big brother nation, which at the time, in the twenties, still occupied and controlled us but also promised to protect us against the Japanese.

I loved my country but could see I'd spend the rest of my life bending and kneeling to pick crops for little money under tropical sun and hard rain that often became typhoons, and said yes, I'd be happy to go to the United States where life would be better. I started in the Central Valley of California, the Golden State, where I moved to Delano and with other Philippine farmworkers, the manongs, traveled up and down to Bakersfield, Santa Maria, Salinas, Stockton, about any place you can name, picking grapes and harvesting carrots and almonds and oranges and a lot more to fill up markets here and have plenty left for wealthy growers to sell other places and get richer. I always stood straight when growers stepped out of their cars on dirt roads next to fields, talking to foremen and pointing, and enjoyed more than resented looking at the faces of power. Sometimes from a distance I looked at their big houses and was impressed to see how people like that lived.

We lived in old boxcars shoved out onto dirt or in sheds and had no plumbing and did most of our business outside. Our pay wasn't good, either, even after 1938 when the federal government passed a minimum wage law of twenty-five cents an hour. We were lucky to get half that, and over the years that's about how it worked, every time there was a minimum wage increase the growers divided by two.

We were even more bothered by laws preventing us from marrying women of other races. I still hear the cutting words: anti-miscegenation. About nine-five percent of us were men, so what were we supposed to do? After work some guys smoked marijuana. I preferred any kind of alcohol we had. We played a lot of cards and boxed and practiced martial arts and played guitars and sang – some of the guys had great voices – and trained our cocks to fight so we could win big bets. The most exciting times came on Saturday nights when we got cleaned up – some camps now had showers – and put on our only suits and slicked down our hair and wedged into old cars a few guys had bought and went to dance halls where we paid for every dance and a lot more later on. Usually, though, there weren't enough girls for the guys and we had to share and any guy who wanted a lady all night had to be ready to fight.

Most of us were small but tough and proud guys who just needed some fun, and we needed someone to organize us. We were ready to challenge the growers but who knows when we would have if Larry Itliong hadn't moved to Delano in the sixties. We'd heard of him. Like many of us he was in his fifties and didn't have much property but at least had a wife, he'd had several wives and children, and thirty years experience organizing workers. He'd started at an Alaskan cannery in the thirties, cut off the middle, ring, and little fingers of his right hand in an accident, and ignored that while helping to found a union up there. In the late forties he was one of the key men behind the asparagus strike near Stockton. He was always trying to get workers contracts and pay equal to the minimum wage and decent working conditions that protected us from pesticides and heat and dehydration.

Larry was a born activist. In an interview I saw a reporter record what I'd heard and seen several times: "I have all kinds of guts. I'm not scared of nobody. I'm a son of a bitch in terms of fighting for the rights of Filipinos in this country. I've got the ability to make people think I'm pretty. At first girls might think I'm ugly but they talk to me for a couple of hours, and I'm pretty."

He could convince people when he talked and smoked his cigar and played cards with us. We trusted him and wanted to follow. In May 1965 he led a strike in Coachella Valley that forced growers to pay higher wages. There were a lot more grapes and Filipinos around Delano. Why shouldn't we also have better pay? On September seventh one thousand five hundred of us picked the top grapes on vines and left those underneath and walked off the job to start our strike.

At a meeting here Larry told our Agricultural Workers Organizing Committee that he'd called Cesar Chavez and said, "We need the support of the National Farm Workers Association."

"We're new and just not ready," Cesar told Larry. "Maybe in two or three years."

"If you don't join our strike, we'll break your next strike."

"We'll vote."

They voted to join us, and we walked the picket lines together and often talked about how strange it was that people so rich wanted to poorly pay people who had so little. We'd vowed to strike as long as we had to, maybe a month or two. A month or two became a year then two, and lots of manongs said they had to eat. Some of the younger guys had brought wives from the Philippines and others, after anti-miscegenation laws were ruled unconstitutional, found wives here, and said they needed to move on to feed their families. I was sixty now and not going to leave. Cesar and Larry and our workers decided to combine organizations and call the new one the United Farm Workers. Cesar became the director and Larry assistant director. Both men traveled and made speeches to raise money to support the strike. When some of our men wanted to hit back at aggressive strikebreakers and their dogs, Cesar went on a fast to emphasize our commitment to nonviolence. He didn't eat for twenty-five days and lost thirty-five pounds and almost died. Bobby Kennedy visited the day the fast ended. And we didn't fight. We kept picketing. Larry and Cesar and countless others spread our word. Many Americans were listening, and finally, in 1970, the growers signed their first union contract with us and offered better pay and benefits.

By this point my body was old and worn out but there was nowhere to work except the fields where I returned. In 1971 Larry Itliong resigned from the UFW, convinced that union practices favored young Mexican Americans over aging Filipinos. I'm not sure. I'm just thankful Larry and Cesar and the UFW built Agbayani Village for old Filipino farmworkers. Almost sixty of us moved there in 1974. I got a small private bedroom, next to a bathroom I shared with the man on the other side, and paid only a hundred and six dollars for the room and all my meals in the large pretty cafeteria and community room where we played cards and remembered the great hard days of our working lives.

Discussion with Cesar Chavez

Thirty miles east of Bakersfield, amid parched brown hills enlivened by dry but green oak trees, in the museum at Cesar Chavez Center, I walk by a replica of a humble room like many farm workers lived in fifty years ago. Walls and the roof are made of thin corrugated metal that sounded like drums under rain and became freezers in winter and ovens in summer. There's a single bed in the corner. That doesn't mean one person lived there. It implies a single sleeping space sufficed for one family or more, often ten people in a cramped room. There's no running water or bathroom. Some workers had worse accommodations, surviving in insect-infested shacks of rotting wood, others in tents. I knock on a tinny wall.

At ten-thirty, as scheduled, a short man with a serene brown face and thick black and gray hair approaches and says, "Good morning, I'm Cesar Chavez."

His handshake is gentle.

"I'm Tom Clark. Thanks for coming."

"You ever live in a place like that?"

"Fortunately, I haven't."

"I lived in plenty and also worked a lot in the fields before I became a community and union organizer. Farm workers respected my background. They knew I was one of them. They know I always will be."

"Your office is in the rear, isn't it?"

"Yes, come on."

The office is closed to the public but visible through a large window revealing a desk covered by papers and folders, and full bookshelves lining two walls.

"Back in the early seventies, you were one of the pioneers in hiring people to build computer systems for your organization, the United Farm Workers. Where's your computer?"

"People designed computer systems for the UFW, but we didn't have personal computers in those days."

"I've read the UFW developed a printing business and did pretty well, and also used mailing lists, from various clients as well as your own rolls, to contact people during political campaigns."

"You must always convey your message."

"Moving back to the sixties, before computers became a factor, you received a lot of favorable coverage for the Delano Grape Strike and your fast in 1968 as well as your association with Bobby Kennedy."

"I also got a lot of bad publicity," Chavez said, "but we knew we were right to strike and boycott products of growers who denied workers even minimum wages and safe working conditions. It took us, and thousands of people helping us around the nation, five years to get a contract."

"There was a lot of violence, on both sides."

"On theirs. We only protected ourselves."

"Respectfully, I think some UFW members, especially your cousin Manuel Chavez, were at times the aggressors. I've just read a biography about you."

I sense some displeasure as Chavez asks, "Which one?"

"*The Crusades of Cesar Chavez* by Miriam Pawel."

"You won't find that one for sale in our bookstore."

"I guess not, but I think her portrayal of you is primarily positive, especially through the early seventies, when you were by far the most important Latino civil rights figure. After that…"

"After that she writes a lot of things that aren't true."

"In that case, why not sue her?"

"I've been gone since 1993 and my family and colleagues don't want to give her any more publicity."

"During your 1968 hunger strike, which lasted twenty-five days, there was a mass every night outside your little room in the old gas station on the UFW's 40 Acres compound in Delano. More than a hundred people came to pray for you."

"Sometimes two or three hundred."

"Do you think some people began to view you as a religious figure, almost a saint, perhaps?"

"No, I don't think so. They viewed me as a man dedicated to bettering their lives. I felt their love."

"That's a lot of adulation for anyone to deal with and keep in perspective," I said. "It seems some of your followers began to worship you."

"I didn't seek to be worshipped. I earned respect for my cause, their cause, of earning a decent wage while working under civilized conditions."

"Your successes in the sixties were remarkable. I think what this biographer, Miriam Pawel, and others are saying is that you isolated yourself here at La Paz, far from the farms in the Central Valley, and spent much less time organizing workers and developing contracts and became, above all, the leader of a commune here on these grounds."

"That's insulting. Ask anyone who really knows. I worked all the time. I ate and slept and worked."

"Some of your allies say you began to view yourself as infallible and demanded absolute power."

"Every leader must have confidence in his judgment. And those who say I ignored my advisors aren't telling the truth. As even this biographer concedes, we had many vigorous arguments here at La Paz. Those discussions, though heated, were democratic in nature. I did have the prerogative of any leader and made final decisions. You see that in corporate America every day. No organization can be completely democratic if it's going to be effective."

"Miriam Pawel, and more importantly those who were here in the seventies, say you were influenced by the Synanon alcohol and drug treatment group, led by Chuck Dederich, that eventually proclaimed itself a religion and forced men to have vasectomies and women to divorce their husbands and mate with those Dederich directed, and I could go on."

"The UFW separated itself from Synanon when it became a bizarre organization and changed its focus from helping people to controlling them."

"But you did adopt their practice of using The Game to control people."

"We didn't use The Game much."

"I'm just quoting those who said they were forced to participate and curse their friends and colleagues and make accusations, many outrageous, that upset and damaged many people."

"There was a lot of good therapy in The Game, but we moved on from it."

"Quite a few longtime colleagues say you arbitrarily ran them off, accusing them of disloyalty, of being assholes, even communists."

"I'm about to run you off now. In forty years as a community organizer, union organizer, and civil rights leader, I came to disagree with some I'd trusted. Perhaps they no longer trusted me, either. Fine. That was their time to move on. I in effect fired some people in a very nonconfrontational way.

"Since you've been trying to ask me tough questions, let me ask you some. Have you ever organized a union? Have you ever organized a boycott? Have you ever attracted thousands of people in your area, and millions nationwide, to a cause that will make their lives better? Have you ever done anything like that? I know you haven't.

"Here, at least read this *Sacramento Bee* article by Bobby Kennedy's daughter, Kerry. You'll see she emphasizes that our efforts for farm workers continued long after the seventies. We've got contracts with Dole and D'Arrigo Brothers, a prominent vegetable grower, and seventy-five percent of California's mushroom industry. Our mushroom workers earn about forty thousand a year and have full health benefits. We also have unionized workers at Gallo and Mondavi wineries. There are plenty of others. Read the article.

"Over the last fifty years, has anyone done more for farm workers than the UFW? I don't think so. Viva la unión. Viva la causa."

CONTRASTS

Crips and Bloods

Next time I drive south from Bakersfield, out of the Central Valley and over snow-glazed Tejon Mountains, I better take a Nat King Cole CD and study his melodic voice so I don't lean to the guy standing next to me on elegant Third Street Promenade in Santa Monica and say, of a slender, suited man singing for tips, "He's lip synching, isn't he?"

"That's live," said the listener.

I would've stayed and tipped the crooner but had to rush around a corner, toward the cool Pacific, to Second Street to see *Crips and Bloods: Made in America.* Two days earlier I'd called Laemmle Theaters, Southern California's champion of independent and foreign films, and asked if any seats remained for the Saturday one p.m. showing. I believed many in the area would be eager to see this documentary and ask the director questions afterward.

"I don't think that'll be a problem, but let me check," the employee said. "So far, none have sold."

I bought a ticket online anyway. At show time some twenty conscientious Caucasians were seated in a theater holding ten times that. Right away we learn in twenty years fifteen thousand people have died from gang-related violence in South Los Angeles. Those numbers crunch into seven hundred fifty deaths a year two a day every day in perpetuity. A tough young man tells the camera he didn't choose his destiny, his destination chose him.

Forest Whitaker narrates a contextual flashback to South L.A. of the 1950's when, though black kids couldn't join the Boy Scouts and their parents were prohibited from buying homes they could've afforded in white neighborhoods, the area was more peaceful. Spurned Boy Scouts joined alternative gangs for a "sense of family, acceptance, status, and safety in numbers." They were competitive with their fists but didn't carry guns. Nowadays the Crips and Bloods often have more firepower than the police.

Righteous William Parker, chief of police from 1950-1966, is recalled as a military-like commander who trained his troops to view young blacks as inferior and the enemy. Many people are interviewed – gang members, ex-members, bereaved mothers, some academics, Jim Brown, and Tom Hayden. Their message: blacks have "internalized self-hatred" and gagged on the "spoonful of hatred" until inevitable eruption. The Watts riots of 1965 are depicted as a result of "one racist traffic stop too many." Two hundred cops, and later the National Guard, were confronted by angry residents and needed five days to suppress flames and protests.

Gang activity was inconsequential from 1965-1971. The civil rights movement galvanized the nation – black Baby Boomers had heroic role models – and factories in the region enabled people to work, buy homes, and raise families. But by the late sixties factories began closing, and Malcolm X, Medgar Evers, Martin Luther King, and numerous Black Panther leaders had been killed, and many others imprisoned. The next generation was thus "born in a state of suspended animation." The Crips stomped into the void, catastrophically replacing Dr. King and his comrades with guys who shoot you for walking into their hood.

Rather than striving to become educated and self-sufficient, the Crips and their rivals, the Bloods, sell crack cocaine and buy automatic weapons and beget many children soon ignored while attacking and counterattacking rival gangs – they kill one of us, we kill two of them – a tragic cycle passed from generation to generation like a hot glass pipe. One in four black males goes to prison. Dad's gone because he sold drugs. Mom gets loaded with the kids. Those who work are said to be too busy to show love to their children.

In 1992 a Simi Valley jury of ten whites, a Latino, and an Asian American – a preposterous venue and jury composition for this trial – freed the police assailants of Rodney King, and enraged blacks swarmed the streets of South L.A, killing fifty-three people, injuring more than two thousand, and burning hundreds of buildings. In the aftermath, many in South L.A. continued to feel whites were signaling "we don't want you, we don't like you, we don't care." Gang warfare intensified. Body counts increased. And post traumatic stress syndrome is now higher for kids here than in Baghdad. A natty and articulate fellow named Kumasi, whose strident voice targets only whites, ends the celluloid travail with this demand: Made In America.

Director Stacy Peralta, a native of Venice Beach, stepped to the front of the theater. About fifteen people stayed to ask what should be done. The highlights: a manufacturing base in the area is essential; kids shouldn't dream only of careers in sports and music; they need jobs besides fast food; those who make it leave South L.A. and with them take vital examples of how to be successful working people; during a year and a half of filming, everyone Peralta talked to had relatives in prison or who'd been shot.

I adjourned to view contemporary art at nearby Bergamot Station, a constellation of about forty upscale galleries, then drove twenty miles east, not to South L.A. but Pasadena, an inland Santa Monica. That evening I watched a dreary Italian film, *Gomorrah,* about Neapolitan gangsters, almost all of whom are white, recently killing four thousand of each other. Overnight I slept badly, didn't exercise Sunday morning, asked myself to go to South L.A., decided to be safe and return to Bakersfield, ate a few pastries and bowls of cereal in the motel office, urged myself to go to the epicenter, resolved to do so, plugged *Hot Rocks* hits by the Rolling Stones into my CD player and headed south on Interstate 110.

I arrived in South Los Angeles about eleven a.m., thinking myself a fool for entering a war zone. What I saw, however, was people living: blacks and Hispanics took Sunday strolls, often by themselves; parents pushed babies in carriages down sidewalks; children with skateboards maneuvered in their driveways; homeowners presided over yard sales; groups talked and laughed on porches; finely-dressed people entered churches.

Mick Jagger bellowed "Street Fightin' Man" and "Sympathy for the Devil" as I cruised middle class neighborhoods with barred doors and windows and lower-middle class areas with the same bars but stronger fences. I knew everything couldn't always be this tranquil – except for those who manufacture and sell bars – but was relieved South L.A. isn't the Battle of Stalingrad. A Spanish-speaking guy selling furniture in front of his house told me he never had problems, the trouble was over there. As we chatted on the sidewalk, an African American man gently placed his hand on my back and said, "Excuse, me." Driving by him a couple of minutes later, I lowered the passenger window, introduced myself and asked for a short interview. He smiled and said, "Sorry, Tom, but I'm too busy now." Feeling good I drove to a church where an hour earlier services were about to commence. Now several men in suits and ladies in dresses stood in the parking lot and watched me pull in and step out, notebook in hand.

"Can I help you?" a man asked.

"Hi, I'd like to talk to a minister."

"Right there," he pointed.

I told a tall husky young man what I wanted, and he agreed.

I recounted my pleasant morning drive.

"The media only shows one side," he said. "If something bad happens, the news reports it and keeps reporting it. Ninety-five percent of what happens is positive. I'll give you an example. When I went to Dorsey High School near here, there was a shooting off campus that didn't involve anyone affiliated with the school. Yet, our school was constantly in the news, and nothing was ever said about our two recent football championships or winning the academic decathlon.

"All big cities have gang violence. Where there's joblessness, there's hopelessness. Now the drug dealing is a bigger problem than the violence. A lot of gangs have set aside their differences – it's all about the money."

"What needs to be done?" I asked.

"There needs to be long-term training. Guys who've never had a job don't know how to act on a job. Even if they had one, they couldn't keep it."

"How is the economic crisis impacting South L.A?"

"Inner cities are always worst hit. Eighteen years ago, long before this crisis, the state closed a youth center over there. That had a negative effect on the community. The center offered basketball, football, art, and music, and was just a positive place to hang out. When it closed, the kids had no place to go.

"Inner city schools are getting hit now. Teachers are laid off, and classes are too large."

I thanked the minister, whose congregants were waiting, and plugged the Stones back in as I drove to 7010 Avalon Boulevard, where I'd toiled in a warehouse right after high school graduation in 1970. It was a miserable damn summer. Air in L.A. was much dirtier then. I don't care if scientific data confirms or refutes this. My eyes are the arbiters, and they never water now but then I almost cried every morning as I swept out driveways where big trucks backed up to the warehouse which is closed, run down, covered with graffiti, and slugged with a sign saying: "Available."

A few minutes later I pulled over near a parked police car. A young male Hispanic officer was sitting on the passenger side. In the driver's seat was a beautiful woman, her long dark brown hair combed back. They smiled bemusedly when I told them what I was doing.

"The problem is there's no daddy and mommy in the home," said the lady. "Basically, kids are having kids."

"The work ethic also needs to improve," the man said. "Everything is given to them. There's jobs out there right now."

"It's the family unit," said the lady. "Too many single parents and no one to watch the kids."

"Thanks."

"Sure," she said. "And be careful out there."

Quito Hills

In Spanish I tell my guide I want to visit some places where the air's clean and the view breathtaking. He says this way and drives from downtown Quito, in the valley, up into mountains around the city to neighborhoods called San Juan, Toctiuco, El Placer and others. Pull over, I frequently say, and step out of the car to proclaim I've never beheld such natural beauty in an urban area: the sky, the mountains, the city below, everything's vivid and alive. The Hollywood Hills by comparison are modest humps above a smog-choked mass; the hills east and west of San Francisco Bay likewise overlook the gray and grim.

There are still quite a few prime lots. They'd cost millions in California. I ask how much they'd be here.

You could probably buy most of these houses, and the lots, for fifty or a hundred thousand, he says.

I'm so invigorated I announce I'm ready to start knocking on doors.

Just a minute, he says. You can't be seduced by the view. Remember, in Latin America the most stunning properties are often ghettoes in the hills above cities. The favelas over Rio de Janeiro and the slums surrounding Caracas are other examples. Look at what's spray painted on the wall over there: Death to the Thieves of the Barrio.

I saw that, I say. But like everyone else I could get a place behind high walls with plenty of glass on top. An alarm system and barred windows would also help.

Most people up here have bars and alarms, he notes, but those things don't do much to improve life. You'd still have to drive into and out of this neighborhood; that's very dangerous, especially at night. The thieves block streets with tires or old furniture or sometimes they just lie in the road. When you stop they'll rob you, at least, using guns or knives or palos, which are wooden clubs. Those guys don't care about anyone. They smoke marijuana or cocaine all day. Some also inject coke. Tonight they'll come out to get more money. Then they'll run into the hills behind these worn houses. The police won't follow them there.

Could I get a gun? Do the people in this community have guns?

No, you can't and no, they don't, he says. Let's drive down the street. I'll show you a billboard. There: Organized Neighborhood Community Alarm. The Quito We Want Is Safe and Supportive.

I'm glad people are helping each other.

They have to, the guide says. Sometimes two or three armed thieves will rob a bus up here. They run up and down the aisles, taking people's cell phones, watches, jewelry, even their shoes.

I point to another community service billboard: Don't Throw Trash. Don't be a Pig. The disreputable animal stands nearby.

There's a two-hundred-dollar fine for throwing trash, he says.

But we've passed dozens of bags of garbage on sidewalks and in the streets.

People bring those out at night, says the guide.

I bet the view is great then, too.

Valley of Cumbaya

Across a Quito street from an elegant hotel where I did not stay, in a Chinese restaurant resembling an antiseptic clinic, a young man introduced himself as the manager and soon revealed that a decade earlier he'd lived in Wyoming a few years.

"That must've been culture shock," I said in English, acknowledging his proficiency outranked mine in Spanish.

"I wanted to go as far from Ecuador as possible," he said.

"Equator to snow drifts, you succeeded."

Rather than tell him the fried rice was greasy and clearly from a package, I mentioned my plan to see one of the residential valleys outside the Ecuadorian capital, and read my list of three.

"Go to Valle de Cumbaya. I was raised there. It's a wonderful place."

I agreed, and back at my economical hotel I hired the bellhop, who'd be off the next day, to drive his car. He'd been genial during my residence and easily convinced me to forgo the services of one of the hotel's regular drivers and pay him ten dollars an hour.

The following morning, in his aging compact car, he asked in Spanish, "Where are we going?"

"El Valle de Cumbaya."

"I thought you wanted to go around the historical center downtown. It's fifteen an hour outside the city."

"Okay, twelve."

"Está bien."

From the high valley floor of Quito, surrounded by the green Andes, he drove several miles down through a canyon into a place much hotter and more severe.

"This is Valle de Cumbaya," he said.

"Let's see some nice houses."

We passed car dealerships and other suburban highlights before cruising numerous streets lined by high concrete walls extended a few more feet by electrified chain-link fencing.

"Is the electricity strong enough to kill?" I asked.

"No, just stop them."
A gate and one or two armed guards fronted every community.
"It's really hot. Does your air conditioner work?"
"Yes," he said, and pushed a button that unleashed air like a heater's.
"I think you need some Freon. Let's head back to Quito."

Looting in Leyte

Don't call me a thief. You might be worse if typhoon waves crushed your wife and kids and flushed them some stinking place I can't find days after looking and not eating or sleeping. I'm not hungry. I'm starving. I can't find any clean water, either, and am vomiting and need medicine for gashes in my face and arms. I want some place where I can turn on a light and take a shower. I have to pull myself together.

I will when I get something to eat in this house. I open the door and see the owner's gun pointed at my stomach and from behind feel a hand grab my shoulder and yank me onto my back outside and watch five guys with guns charge in. I get up and walk streets I don't recognize.

Come with us, says a man in a group of dozens. We're going to the rice warehouse.

I should've remembered. Thousands are already there. Guards can't stop them. They're gone. Maybe they're eating rice. That's what we need. Everyone moves forward in a human tidal wave. We break the fence, smash doors, jump through windows, we knock down walls and hear screams of people dying, people who won't get our rice. Thousands, tens of thousands of bags are being hauled outside. Several times I try to get mine but am knocked down. I keep attacking and wish I had a gun. I'd kill the next guy who stops me. There's a bag. That one's mine. I grab it but can barely lift. A week ago I could've easily carried two. I wrestle this one up to my waist and almost faint pulling it onto my shoulder but I've got it. Now, where will I go and how will I cook it and what about thieves?

Foxxconn Opportunities

It may be a secret some places but the Chinese know many kids young as twelve leave no heat or plumbing villages and ride migratory buses to work for great technology firm Foxconn which gets several thousand applications daily from those anxious to be paid promptly albeit modestly and live in huge heated dormitories and enjoy promised spare time to swim play chess climb mountains and fish.

Perhaps it's exciting at first to live with three hundred thousand eager employees making lives better but hard to learn no talking even during brief breaks or accept militaristic bosses shouting and writing black marks on records so workers will focus on production and remember America needs millions of devices that must be made by hands moving same way thousands of times daily during seventy-hour weeks crippling carpal tunnel hands that can't continue making brilliant products too expensive to buy anyway. Workers don't say much or are replaced by hordes moving in for fifteen thousand workers who quit each month.

Really they never have time to catch fish or climb mountains and realize there's only a pool or two for everyone but most decide not to jump into mobs standing in sewer water instead they return to dorm roof and realize if concerned bosses had hung nets sooner many coworkers would've landed softly.

Harvest of Shame

As the documentary begins, I, Edward R. Murrow, am smoking a cigarette. I look a bit like Bogart but am not an actor. I'm the most famous radio and television journalist of my era and have been celebrated since my compelling World War II descriptions of Hitler's bombs falling on Britain emboldened millions to believe in ultimate victory. In 1954 in the still-new medium of television I took on Senator Joseph McCarthy and helped reveal him as a self-aggrandizing hypocrite more interested in fabricating communist conspiracies than protecting the United States. Now, in 1960, from Florida and elsewhere in the richest nation on earth, I present *Harvest of Shame* launched by a farmer's statement: "We used to own slaves; now we rent them."

Who are these almost-slaves a hundred years after the Civil War? They're migrant farm workers, white and black, and my staff and I talk to and film many of them. Here's a woman, age thirty-four, who has nine children. They get milk once a week. On good nights they may share a pot of beans, or some fried potatoes, or a little boiled corn. She doesn't think they'll ever get more.

Next there's a little boy caring for his brothers and sisters. Rats have eaten a hole in his bed. His mother is twenty-nine years old and has thirteen other children. She started working in the fields when she was eight. Now she toils from six a.m. to four p.m. and earns about what it takes to feed the family that day. When finished harvesting in one area, she and other pickers must immediately vacate shanties so owners save electricity. The mother doesn't think she'll ever escape.

For migrant workers a dollar or two after basic expenses seems like "all the money in the world," and they'll have to struggle for that. While the produce they've harvested moves rapidly in trains or refrigerated trucks, migrant workers travel less comfortably than cattle, riding in trucks that sometimes don't stop for ten hours. At the next shanty the owners supply straw instead of beds. There are no bathrooms. One owner says the workers are happy because they have no worries; they're the happiest people in the world. He does concede they make a poor living. Mrs. Brown began this cycle when she was eight-years old. Thirty years later, she does not see a way out.

On June sixth, 1957, nine miles from Fayetteville, North Carolina, twenty-one Negro workers jammed into a flat-bed truck were killed in a head-on collision. When there are not enough Americans for this life, farmers recruit braceros from Mexico and the Caribbean. Regardless of origin, many migrant workers cannot afford to stay in labor camps. Presumably they sleep outside. Families in camps share a single room. Bachelors get a bunk in the bull pit. None of the workers has a place as well-appointed as nearby stables for special horses. In New York State there is a camp where children receive a half-pint of milk and one cracker each while parents work up to seventy miles away. Owners brag about offering modest benefits and, naturally, they oppose unions, strikes, and federal legislation that would change their system.

I stop inhaling my cigarette, which I can't comfortably forgo more than twenty minutes, and emphasize hope lies with education of the migrant workers' six hundred thousand children. Most leave school before age sixteen, and only one in five thousand finishes high school. No one recalls a college graduate. Lack of desire is not the problem. One teacher emphasizes the kids are anxious to get an education, but laments it's difficult for those from very large families in rural areas to go further than junior high. Farmers say they can't help by paying more since they're competing with farmers from others states. Housing must also be poor since owners won't build something nice to use only six weeks a year.

Secretary of Labor James Mitchell says he's sad because the migrant workers have no voice in Congress while their employers do. Mitchell is frustrated by his inability to make any regulations; it's morally wrong to exploit workers, and we should not tolerate it; but Lord help anyone who suggests doing something for the workers.

At the end of harvests in the North, buses and trucks take migrant workers South to start the process again. They're broke when they leave and broke when they return and at the mercy of weather. If there's a drought, they'll stand in bread lines since they're ineligible for unemployment benefits. Secretary Mitchell and a small group in Congress have recommendations for those who have no lobby: extend Child Labor laws; make migrant workers eligible for health, education, and welfare programs; enact a federal law requiring crew leaders to register; extend workman's compensation to agriculture; enact new housing laws; mandate that states pay local school boards for education of migrant children.

These recommendations enrage farm owners who claim such government interference would be socialism. I disagree. I believe those who have the strength to harvest fruit and vegetables but not the strength to protect themselves need strong government. Maybe others can help. Good night, and good luck, I say.

Notes: CBS Reports broadcast *Harvest of Shame* the day after Thanksgiving 1960. Edward R. Murrow's critiques of the establishment put him in conflict with CBS president William S. Paley who had already cut back Murrow's air time and relegated him to an unfavorable Sunday afternoon slot. Murrow resigned from CBS and in 1961 accepted President John F. Kennedy's offer to head the United States Information Agency. He died of lung cancer in April 1965, two days after his fifty-seventh birthday. Humphrey Bogart had died of the same disease, at the same age, several years earlier.

Sources (In Other Hands)

Interviews

I appreciate the interviews granted by prostitutes, detectives, social workers, taxi drivers, and others in such diverse places as Bakersfield, Pasadena, Mexico City, Aguascalientes, Managua, San Jose (Costa Rica), and Madrid.

I also had helpful conversations with members of the Magdalene Hope Ministry, Michael Fagans, director of *The Trafficked Life*, Stephany Powell, a retired vice detective and current director of Journey Out, and Donald Loomis, whose varied jobs have, at times, allowed him to speak to those in the sex trade.

Symposiums and Lectures

"Trade of Innocents," Bakersfield, October 2012. Blom, Jeff; Cisneros, Diana. Interview on phone with Jeff Blom on February 4, 2016.

Books

Clark, George Thomas. From the collection *The Bold Investor:* "The Pink Zone" is an excerpt from the short story "Zona Rosa."

Tabor, Pauline. *Pauline's – Memoirs of the Madam on Clay Street.*

Movies

Born into Brothels, directed by Zana Briski and Ross Kauffman.

Never on Sunday, directed by Jules Dassin.

Trade of Innocents, directed and written by Christopher Bessette.

The Trafficked Life, directed by Michael Fagans.

Sources (Where Will We Sleep?)

Interviews

I learned much by talking to campesinos, laborers, teachers, taxi drivers, homeless people, and others in places as different as Bakersfield, Lamont, Delano, Pasadena, Mexico City, Aguascalientes, Managua, San Jose (Costa Rica), Quito, and Madrid.

Thanks to the The Mission at Kern County – it was once known as The Rescue Mission – for permitting me to visit their facility numerous times over more than a decade and interview program residents and homeless dinner guests for the stories "Christmas Eve," "New Year's Eve," and "Cycle of Abuse," and participate in their census taking one year and witness events that formed the story "Homeless on the River."

Symposiums and Lectures

"Bold Step: A celebration of the 50th Anniversary of the Delano Grape Strike" in September 2015 at Robert F. Kennedy High School in Delano and an interview with John Itliong, one of Larry Itliong's seven children.

Lectures about Cesar Chavez and the Delano Grape Strike, at CSU Bakersfield in September 2015, by Dolores Huerta, Miriam Pawel, and Matt Garcia.

Books

Pawel, Miriam. *The Crusades of Cesar Chavez*

Movies

Harvest of Shame, directed by Fred W. Friendly and starring Edward R. Murrow.

About the Author

George Thomas Clark is the author of twelve books including *They Make Movies, Hitler Here*, an internationally-acclaimed biographical novel, *The Bold Investor, Paint it Blue, Basketball and Football, Obama on Edge*, and *Down Goes Trump*.

Clark also follows the news and sports, exercises daily (albeit delicately), collects contemporary art, enjoys independent movies, and travels to places (most recently Madrid, Mexico City, Quito, Guanajuato, and Aguascalientes) where he can socialize in Spanish.

The author's website is GeorgeThomasClark.com

www.ingramcontent.com/pod-product-compliance
Lightning Source LLC
Chambersburg PA
CBHW032127170626
46808CB00006B/2135